FORGIVEN

THE NASH BROTHERS, BOOK TWO

CARRIE AARONS

Copyright © 2019 by Carrie Aarons

All rights reserved.

No part of this book may be reproduced in any form or by any electronic or mechanical means, including information storage and retrieval systems, without written permission from the author, except for the use of brief quotations in a book review.

This is a work of fiction. Names, characters, businesses, places, events and incidents are either the products of the author's imagination or used in a fictitious manner. Any resemblance to actual persons, living or dead, or actual events is purely coincidental.

Editing done by Proofing Style.

Cover designed by Okay Creations.

Do you want your **FREE** Carrie Aarons eBook?

All you have to do is **sign up for my newsletter**, and you'll immediately receive your free book!

To anyone who has waited a very long time for love to be requited.

1

LILY

Smoke pours out from under the hood of my car, and a clap of thunder has me gently banging my forehead against the steering wheel.

"Why now?" I groan, asking the universe why my karma has gone from zilch to double zilch in the last ten minutes.

Of course, my brand new vehicle is breaking down on the side of the road right as it's about to storm. What a perfect metaphor for my life.

Okay, it's not that bad, I'm just being dramatic. But I'm tired after smiling and shaking hands at one of my father's rallies across county lines, and all I want to do is curl up on the oversized couch in my townhouse living room with the most recent romance novel I checked out. Now, it looks like I'll be waiting for a tow truck instead of pulling on yoga pants.

The sky splits in a flash of light, right down the center, and not three seconds later does a boom from the heavens seem to shake the earth below my tires. The rain is threatening, and I dig in my bag for my phone to call Johnny at the garage I regularly use in Fawn Hill.

But the line just rings and rings, and either he's talking to every single resident of my small hometown, or I'm out of range. It's probably the latter, and I have to suck in a shaky breath to keep from crying.

Today has been trying. This week has been trying. Hell, the last ten years of my life have been trying. That's just how it goes when you are nowhere near where you expected to be at this age. At one time in my life, I thought by twenty-eight, I'd be married with two children, watching from the stands as the only man I ever loved—

I have to mentally shut the images flooding my brain down. Now the tears do come, sharp and brutal, stinging my face just as equally as they're stinging my heart. How, after all these years, I can still be such a mess over him ... it's the cruelest act of fate I've ever seen.

But, I'm a big girl now. I have my dream job; I run a local government entity, own my townhouse and have friends who love me for me. And hey, I negotiated with a car salesman last week to get this car down five thousand dollars in price. It may be malfunctioning now, but I'd worked hard to both save for this car and advocate for myself.

So, remembering that, I swallow my emotion and call every garage or tow company within a twenty-five-mile radius. As I dial, the car gets worse; the smoke wafting over the hood and the smell of burning stinging my nostrils. I get out of the car, just in case it blows up, and continue my quest for a tow.

I'm on garage number ten, whose voicemail I get when headlights come beaming in my direction. Another car! Thank heavens. My car broke down on a back road that even locals don't normally use, but I like the shortcut back from Lancaster ... and it's a bit like driving down memory lane.

The vehicle approaching is a truck, one of those monster things with tires as big as my torso and a bed that you could fit an entire football team into. Nighttime is fast upon us, and I can't make out the color as dusk sets in, but who cares.

I flag it down, attempting to point to my smoking car just in case the driver doesn't realize that I'm stranded out here. It's not likely that anyone from this part of Pennsylvania *won't* stop, but occasionally, you'll get a jerk or two.

The truck slows down, and my heart rate instantly picks up.

Because I know this truck.

Not intimately, it's been far too long for him to still have the same pickup he drove in high school. But I've seen it around town. It haunts my periphery, and whenever I spot it, I try to stay far away from it.

The driver cuts the engine, and then there he is. Climbing out in all of his giant, muscled glory.

My knees go weak, my mouth runs dry, my heart shakes unsteadily.

Bowen Nash has always been the most gorgeous male specimen in my opinion; I never could take my eyes off of him. From the first time I saw him my freshman year of high school, the big, bad baseball-playing sophomore whose smile could charm a viper ... every other guy ceased to exist.

But at this moment? He was a man in every sense of the word. And my lord, no man had ever done it better.

Broad, muscled shoulders led to arms thickly roped with hard-earned biceps and forearms. His chest alone was probably as long as my wingspan, and it led to a tapered waist where I imagined the steel-cut abs were smattered with hair darker than the close-cut fade that adorned his head. Not that I'd seen them in a very long time, but ...

Now he's walking toward me, those massive, sculpted thighs pressing against the fabric of his jeans as he maneuvers like a jungle cat. Bowen has always had that unteachable swagger to him.

I'm scared to look up into his face because that's the part that hooks my heart like a fish waiting to meets its doom. Powerless, that's what I am. The man's avoided me for ten years, and yet, if he confessed his love for me tomorrow, I'd go running back.

Sucking in a breath, I finally meet those blue eyes. The ones that gazed at me as we danced at prom. Those cerulean, almost translucent blue eyes that watched as I gave myself to him and only him, for what I thought would be forever. Bowen's eyes had looked at me through all the most important moments of our young lives ... and now, he barely swung them my way.

"Oh." He stops short once he sees it's me that he's jumped out of his chariot to rescue.

What he meant to say is, "Oh, it's you," but the disdain in his tone still gets his message across.

I'm not sure where it all went wrong. My memories of that time are still fuzzy. All I do know is that we crashed and burned, both physically and in our relationship. And I ended up losing the love of my life for reasons he still won't reveal.

"My car broke down," I offer weakly, stating the obvious because I don't know what else to say.

Bowen looks at the smoking hood and walks past me, not even a flicker of kindness thrown my way. He pops the hood and disappears. After a few seconds, I round it, not able to stand here in his presence if he won't even speak to me.

"It's fine, I'm calling for a tow. You can go."

He ignores me. "I'm not a mechanic, but I'd say your radiator is busted. Is this ... someone else's car?"

The way he says it, he might as well ask if I'm seeing someone because his tone is so accusatory. As if he'd even care, which is the strangest part.

"It's new. I bought it last week."

"Someone took advantage of you." Bowen's gaze is unimpressed.

This treatment makes me want to cry as does almost every interaction with my ex-boyfriend. From high school sweethearts to practical strangers ... it was tragic.

And in this instance, it was getting old. Jeez, it was far past old. It was ancient.

"I said, I'm fine. I'll handle it. You don't want to help, so go." My tone has more bitterness in it than I thought I could possibly direct toward him.

Just as the words leave my mouth, the first of the rain starts to fall. Steadily pattering down onto us and the cars, I hold a hand up to cover my head. It does nothing, however, to remediate the sputtering under the hood of my car.

Bowen looks at the smoke, at me, and up at the rainy sky ... and sighs loudly.

"I can give you a ride."

No please, no real caring about the statement, no courtesy. "Yeah ... I think I'll pass."

My sarcasm must have pissed him off. "Get in the car, *Lily*."

The nails digging into my palms bite with pain. "I said I'm fine. Don't do me any favors, *Bowen*."

Overhead, the sky cracks with lightning, one I can almost feel the electricity of on my face.

"I'm not leaving you out here to fry. Or worse, drown. Get in the car. I won't be the one blamed if you die."

His words shock us both to stillness ... and I realize he didn't think about what he was saying until it was already coming out of his mouth.

Because once upon a time, he *had* almost killed me.

I move before I can think again, running to the passenger side of his truck. Bowen follows, a burly figure getting soaked as he angrily stomps through the rain.

The rain sluices the windshield as we drive in silence, the wipers batting it quickly, only for the watery curtain to appear seconds later. It might be cold and damp outside, but inside the cab of the truck, the humidity of our attraction, the chemical way we've always been pulled to each other ... it's scorching me.

This night isn't unlike that night ten years ago, the one that changed both of our courses forever. Rain, lightning, darkness closing in and country roads that bend too easily. Him in the driver's seat, me in the passenger seat. Some old Tim McGraw song on the radio.

Except we weren't those kids anymore, the ones who were wild and in love and thought the world couldn't tell them boo. Those teenagers had their whole lives ahead of them, and they expected to be living them together.

"Thank you," I croak out.

The truck passes the sign for Fawn Hill, Bowen navigating us through town. He ignores my sincerity. "You still stay with your parents?"

Of course, he wouldn't know that I bought my own place, finally, last year. We don't know each other anymore.

"No, I have a townhouse on Conover." I smile.

"I know the development." He hasn't looked at me since we got in the car.

Part of me was hoping he'd say he was proud of me, that he'd always believed I could be independent of my political father. But, like always, he says nothing.

Fawn Hill is deserted, most people are sitting down around the dinner tables with their families at this time. I take advantage of the darkness that's set in ... to stare at Bowen as he drives.

The set of his cheekbones, his eyebrows, his jaw ... they're all filled with so much fury.

As he pulls the car onto the one lane road that leads around the circle of my townhouse community, I direct him to a stop just outside my door.

When he only grunts a goodbye, I melt.

I forget that I wasn't the only one who lost everything in that accident.

My hand reaches for his face, my fingertips feeling over the rough of his barely there beard. It's more like a five-o'clock shadow and is the exact same shade of the neat cut of his locks. The move must shock Bowen because his head whips around, and the minute his eyes lock onto mine, I'm clued in on the tiniest shred of vulnerability.

He's opened the door just a crack, and I search his expression, finding only pain, and it breaks my heart open. Bowen always seems to know how to make my heart weep.

"I'll say it for the thousandth time, but I hope you hear me. I don't know what it is I did to make you hate me so much, but I'm sorry."

I slide out of the passenger seat and slam the truck door in frustration. The prickly sense of old scar tissue being cut open again stays with me for the rest of the week.

2

BOWEN

The throbbing in my collarbone aches like a thousand painful memories past.

Fawn Hill's recent down-pouring of rainstorms isn't good for the scar tissue that runs rampant through the healed injury, and I could probably say the same for my heart.

I open the blinds on my barbershop windows, fat drops from the sky coating them and leaving Main Street a blur beyond the glass.

Thank God the library isn't on Main Street. It's closer to the elementary school, set off the main couple of roads in Fawn Hill, and I'm an appreciative bastard for that. If I had to look across the street every day and see her, I might go mad.

Hell, I was already halfway to insane. I lived in the same town that my high school sweetheart and I had grown up in ... and she still lived here, too. I was at the mercy of every person in this town who could still feel the undeniable chemistry between Lily Grantham and me and whispered about it as we passed.

Lily Grantham.

Fuck, did it have to be her on the side of the road? What the hell was the world trying to do to me?

And why can't I get the feel of her touch on my cheek out of my heart, my head, and scrubbed from my skin?

Her smell still lingers in my truck. Every time I've gotten in the thing for the last four days, I can smell the lavender mixed with warm vanilla ... the scent she's worn for years. I don't even know the perfumes name, or I'd have probably bought myself a bottle before now. To smell in the sanctity of my home like some weird serial killer.

Really, I just missed her more than fucking anything.

Lily had always been tiny. She was smaller than petite ... her lithe, tight body was something out of Neverland. I'd always been a giant, and she'd been the pixie that fit perfectly in my lap.

How I wished I could have lost control in that car, pulled her on top of me and felt those small curves under my hands again. Since we'd been together, Lily had become a woman. Over the last ten years, I had to avert my eyes not to notice the sway in her hips, the way her perfectly round tits show a hint of cleavage in those buttoned-up tops she wears.

And my God, the black-rimmed glasses she dons for work? I've had to duck around a corner one too many times to banish my erection in public.

The long brown hair that used to curl around my fingers when I made love to her. The midnight blue eyes that looked up at me, full of so much love.

How could I even exist on this planet if those things weren't mine anymore?

But I'd made a promise, and it had kept me from her for ten years. One measly ride in a car, her fingertips on my jaw ... it wasn't going to undo all that.

A couple of customers filter in and out through the morning, but it's a Thursday and business is slower. The weekend will pick up, but I have a good gig going here, as the town's only barbershop.

Not that this is what I ever envisioned myself doing as a career. I thought I'd be well into a major league baseball career by this time, touring the country, playing in all the stadiums I revered as a kid.

That night ten years ago changed way more than just my relationship with Lily.

My life could always be worse. I owned my own business, had no one to answer to, fought fires when I was needed. The firefighting came about in a strange way, but the town needed more volunteers, and cutting hair wasn't exactly exciting. I wanted the rush again, and that's what it provided.

But ... I wasn't necessarily happy. Those trophies and honors and plaques, they all sat in my basement, collecting dust. Sometimes, just to rub more salt in the gaping wound, I'd watch my baseball tapes, the ones Dad had made when I was trying to get scouted for college.

In another life, I would be under those lights, in front of TV cameras, winning a World Series. The fact that I wasn't doing that ... it crushed me more than I even knew how to express in words.

The bell over the door to my shop jingles, and I look up from where I'm wiping down a counter of one of the four stations in the place.

Keaton sits down in my chair, and I walk over, swing a cape around his shoulders.

"Been busy today?" He starts off, feigning small talk.

I know my brother better than I know myself. He's my best friend and the worst liar in the world. The guy is just too honest for faking anything.

"Couple customers. Good for a Thursday. But that's not why you're here."

"I'm here for a haircut." My brother smiles at me in the mirror hanging above my station.

I grit my teeth. "Out with it, Keat."

He sighs, relenting just as I begin to buzz the nape of his neck. "Someone saw you dropping Lily off a couple of days ago. It's around town that you two were in your truck together."

Fuck Fawn Hill and its rampant gossip line. These were some of the nosiest people in the world, I swear. My lips stay clamped, my breath coming in furious snorts as I work over my brother's scalp.

After a few minutes of silence, Keaton speaks.

"Bowen, you know why this is a bad idea ..."

I throw my electric razor onto the tabletop of my station. "You don't think I know that? Her car broke down on that back road in from Lancaster. The old farmer's service road. What was I going to do, Keat, leave her there in a thunderstorm?"

That shuts him up, and I pick up my scissors to trim the longer ends.

"I'm not sure I want you with scissors anywhere near my face right now. I am proposing tomorrow, you know."

I did know ... he's only told me seven hundred times. I try to wipe the salty expression off my face. I like Presley. I like her a hell of a lot. But I find it hard to get excited about anything that concerns love or marriage anymore.

Probably because mine was decapitated before it could even really get the chance to thrive.

Keaton clears his throat. "That was nice of you. I know how hard that ride must have been."

Nodding, I try to focus on my work. "Toughest thing I've done in almost three years."

I'm referencing Dad's death, and the grieving that we were *still* going through, and Keaton knows it.

"Bow ..." Keaton's eyes stare at me in the mirror, waits until he knows he has my attention. "I need you to be on your best behavior tomorrow. You know Lily is going to be there, and whatever the other night was about ... I need you to put a lid on it for now. For me. For Presley."

Annoyance buzzes around me like a fly I want to swat. "You don't think I'm going to be as civil as possible tomorrow? Obviously, I'm not going to mess anything up for you. I'm kind of offended you even had to say anything."

He shrugs. "I know that when it comes to Lily ... you can go a little crazy sometimes."

I'm not sure what he's talking about. Unless maybe he's alluding to the two times over the last year that I've punched holes in my wall after having to be within five feet of my ex-girlfriend.

Not that I hated Lily ... fuck, it was the exact opposite. Being around her, having to ride in the same truck cab as her, feeling those dark denim eyes on me ... it tore me apart. Seeing her reminds me of everything we should have had, and all the things that will never be.

Being in her presence is physical torture ... all I want to do is touch her. Hold her. Unravel her in only the way I know how ... in the way that was only ever supposed to come from me. It's like a knife to the heart knowing that another man has probably touched her by now. When I think about it, I get nauseous.

Not that I have any right to feel that way. I've been with other women ... mostly trying to forget about her. It's never worked, and I've always felt worse after.

I sigh, tired of talking. Even to my brothers, more than a couple minutes of conversation and I'm physically exhausted. One time, my mom told me I was an introvert, and it wasn't until years later that I looked up the definition. And realized that the reason I can barely stand to talk to a loved one, much less a stranger, for half a second is that it does physically take its toll on me.

My body shuts down, and aggravation takes over the energy

flowing through me. I can't explain it, only to say that I don't people well. I never have. Sure, I can bring the charm or friendliness if I really feel like it, but most of the time, I'd rather sit in my house alone than talk to someone else. Being from a big family has forced me to adapt in the course of my lifetime, but it's still my natural instinct.

"I won't let you down, brother. Whatever you need my help with, I'm here for you." Because I am.

Even if it will gut me to stand in the same room as Lily while my brother gets engaged.

3
LILY

I'm standing in the middle of my worst nightmare.

A Nash brother is down on one knee, in front of all of *my* closest friends, asking the woman he loves to be his wife and spend forever with him.

She is smiling at him through tears, so much hope and love on her face it's touching the souls of everyone in the room.

That is, except for mine.

Sure, I smile, say "awwww" when everyone else does as Keaton pulls out a velvet box and presents it to Presley. I even cheer when she says yes and they begin to kiss. But inside, I'm dying.

Certainly, I'm happy for Presley, the woman who's become a very good friend since she walked into my library. And I can separate those feelings of love and excitement for her from the ones swirling inside my gut.

Sorrow, so much that it overflows in my blood, pierces through me. Because ... I always thought this would be us someday. Bowen and I, returning to Fawn Hill after the baseball season wrapped up. Him getting down on one knee inside the gazebo in Bloomsbury Park. *Our* gazebo.

He'd ask me to marry him, and I'd dissolve into a puddle of sobs as I said yes. As all our dreams came true. We'd put an announcement in the paper and get married in the church I'd attended as a girl. I'd walk down the aisle to him, being his and his only.

That dream is long gone though, for him and for me. I won't pretend I haven't been with another man out of spite, and I can't turn a blind eye to the floozies he's paraded in and out of the Goat & Barrister for a decade.

We're ruined, both for each other and other people. Shells of the heart-eyed teens we used to be.

Once upon a time that would have been me standing in front of a kneeling Nash man. But not anymore.

"You okay?" Penelope turns to me, whispering.

Tears glisten in her bright green eyes, and I know that I'm not the only one in the room mourning what should have been.

I hug her tight, our embrace a coverup gesture. To the outside observer, we're just so happy that our best friend is getting married. But the secret between the two of us is that watching that proposal was like taking a bullet. For me, because the love of my life was standing in the same room, hating me. And for her, thinking about the husband who was now buried in the cemetery five miles away from where she and her kids went to visit him.

Penelope sighs against me and we finally let go, knowing that when we do, we'd better have our best poker faces on.

"Oh, my goodness!" Presley holds up her hand to show us, and we both nod emphatically, smiles at mega-watt volume.

I am truly happy for her. She and Keaton have been through their struggles, both together and separately, and deserve to come out on the winning end.

But, I need a minute. I walk to the back of Presley's brand new yoga studio, a place I feel like I'll now be spending a lot of time at. I grab a plastic flute of champagne that someone passes me and sip it as I walk along the mirrored wall.

Inspecting my reflection, I try to see beneath the petite, brunette librarian that everyone always says is, "so pretty and intelligent ... a real nice girl."

Before I know what's happening, Bowen has cornered me in. Not wanting to make a scene, I stand there, his sullen eyes watching me.

"What happened the other night ..."

I cut him off, so sick of his wrath. "I know. You're going to say it can't happen again. I get it, Bowen. You don't want me anywhere near you. I've only been getting the message loud and clear for ten years now, thanks."

"I don't hate you."

And then my world stops turning. Noises bounce off my ears, but I don't hear them. The hair on my skin stands on end with the awareness of his body close to mine. My eyes water from not blinking, from the sheer shock of his statement.

"I don't know why you'd think that."

It starts turning again, fury busting full force out of my chest.

"Um ... what? You don't understand why I'd think you hated me? Bowen ... you've avoided me for ten years. Oh, and before that, you broke up with me with a mere text after I'd just woken up from a coma. Every time we're in the same room, the sneers and disgust rolling off you somehow tipped me off to your loathing me. Please, don't stand there and lie through your teeth."

Now it's his turn to be shocked. I've never really talked back to him, not in the decade we've been broken up. Also, neither of us has ever brought up our breakup or the accident so bluntly. Come to think of it, I don't think we've *ever* talked about them.

Sure, there were the first few months I was healthy enough to hunt him down ... this was about six months after the accident. But by that point, he was in a technical school after he could no longer play baseball. He'd moved an hour away, and after the year he'd done that, he went to a firefighting training camp closer to Lancaster. I barely saw him in the two years after he flipped us in a car and shattered our life together.

It wasn't as if I hadn't tried though. As often as I could sneak away without my father catching on to where I was going, I'd try to get to Bowen. I'd either seek him out, leave letters under his windshield wipers, email him from fake accounts that my parents wouldn't notice. It sounds stalker-ish now that I say it out loud, but we were *in love*. And there was absolutely no closure.

Maybe that's why I've never been able to move on with my life.

Bowen's glower intensifies. He's always worn that broody glare, but for me, when we were together, it used to have a layer of smoldering painted into it. When he looked at me, all those years ago, I could literally combust on the spot. Bowen Nash was bad boy charm personified, and we lived fast and loose together. Him, the cocky baseball player who'd fallen for the good girl, and me, the innocent pixie he'd spun around his finger.

"I ... I don't mean to be like that. It's just ... life moves on. I don't want our bad blood tainting Keaton and Presley's engagement, or marriage."

"As if I'd ever do anything to spoil their happiness. You know me, at least give me that," I say quietly.

Bowen looks down at his boots. "I know you wouldn't."

It's the kindest thing he's said to me since we stopped being us.

We're interrupted when Presley comes bounding over, and I slap a smile on my face even though I feel like crying. "Oh my goodness, congratulations! I'm so happy for you two!"

She embraces me hard, and I try to give her the same enthusiasm back.

"I can't even believe this. On my soft opening, too! You guys knew all along, didn't you?" She gleams.

I look at Bowen, nodding. "Guilty. Keaton wanted help to make it a total surprise. You deserve it!"

Presley hip bumps Bowen. "You helped? Damn, I'm surprised, brother. A declaration of love in a yoga studio ... and Bowie was in on it? Pigs really must be flying."

"I told you, don't call me that." He bares his teeth at her.

I chuckle because she's started to call him by the nickname Fletcher dubbed him with.

"Well, any who, I know it's super early, but I just can't help myself. Technically, it's been like five seconds since we got engaged. Remember that? And I know I can speak for Keaton when I say he wouldn't mind me asking. So ... will you be our best man and maid of honor?"

Someone probably needs to get an ambulance over here and check my pulse. Because I'm pretty sure I'm flatlining.

Hopefully, I've managed to wipe the look of horrification that my mind is sure reads all over my expression off of my face.

Because how the hell am I going to organize a wedding with the love of my life, who no longer loves me?

How the hell am I going to stand across an altar from the man I was supposed to be standing there with?

4

BOWEN

"I don't understand why Keaton chose you to be his best man?"

Fletcher throws the ball at me, my glove catching it with a nice thud that ripples the leather covering my hand.

After the last rainy week of May, we're finally into the warm June sunshine, and it's the first chance we've gotten to come out and toss a ball around. Even if baseball isn't my career, it's still my passion. My fingers itch to touch that first hint of leather and laces as soon as April comes around, and the World Series is like a religious holiday in the Nash household.

Growing up, all of us played. Keaton was decent while Fletcher and Forrest had fun with it but weren't ever really serious players. I, on the other hand, ate, slept, and bled the sport. I had been a shortstop; I was quick on my feet, could react in a split second, and whipped that ball so hard when I needed to make a play that scouts called me a dynamite. My bat was just as hot as my hand.

All that disappeared the night of the accident though. After the crash, the doctors discovered I'd broken my right arm, my throwing arm, in three places. My collarbone had a number of breaks and fractures. I'd almost punctured my lung, sprained my tailbone, and fractured my left ankle. I was a fucking mess for a while after that night, and even though everything properly healed and I'd done every inch of rehab asked of me ...

I just wasn't the same. The game didn't click for me like it had before. My mind knew how to move, my heart still had the same passion, but my body was sluggish. The control I'd once exerted over my arm and hand wasn't there anymore. My timing was off, I could no longer hit the way I once had.

For eighteen years, I'd harbored a dream. And in one night, I robbed *myself* of it.

The thoughts eat me alive daily, so I box them up, choosing to compartmentalize instead of talking about the rage. If a team came calling, I'd pack up my things, sell the barbershop and never look back. But that was a pipe dream ... even if it had been hammering on my brain harder than ever since Keaton had proposed.

His moving on seemed to spark something in me. What was I doing? I lived in a town that was the epitome of my worst nightmare, cutting hair and fighting fires. Not because I particularly liked to, but because I was average at it and it made me good money. Was that really the kind of life to live?

I wind up, aiming for Forrest, who stands at the plate holding a bat. He whacks the air, connecting with a piece of the ball, but not the full meat of it so that it soars. Fletcher jogs about twenty feet to catch it, and it lands in his glove. He holds his closed fist up and smiles.

"Got it. You suck, Forrest!" he taunts his twin.

I chuckle, just glad to be out on the field again, even if it is little league size.

"Shut the fuck up, Fletch. If Bowen wasn't actually pitching at me, I'd be able to hit. Ease up, old man." He points at me with his bat.

"Can't help it that you're the worst out of all of us," I half-joke.

"Yeah, clearly Keaton sees you as the best man." Fletch sulks again as he tosses the ball back.

I toss it to him, playing a little catch, while I talk. "Oh, come on, Fletch. You two will be each other's best men, and Keaton asked me to be his with the intention of him being mine someday. Not that it will happen, but we've all got each other covered."

Fletcher nods, looking at Forrest. "You better ask me to be your best man, or I'll give you an Indian burn so hard, your arm will catch fire."

These two are actual children. Seriously ... they're practically children compared to me. Four years might not seem like much, but they're the babies of the family and have always been treated as such. They're goofballs, troublemakers, and general pains-in-my-ass.

Mostly Forrest, whose mouth and brains land him in hot water more times than I can count on a daily basis. But Fletcher is the one I worry about. He's the brother who keeps me up at night, the one whose name I listen for on my firefighter-issued police scanner. He's almost ten months sober, and he's doing great. But before this? He was a mess.

"Don't worry, dipshit, I'll be your best man. But I won't ask you. Not because I wouldn't, but fuck no am I getting married." Forrest makes a face as if he's just sucked on a lemon.

"Why not?" I'm curious as I lob him an easy pitch, and he thwacks it, sending Fletcher running after the nice hit.

My reasoning for never having to ask Keaton to be my best man is that I won't ever love a woman the way I love Lily. Why would I get married if my whole heart wasn't in it? I've never thought marriage and a family were stupid ... as I suspect Forrest does. I just know it's no longer in the cards for me.

Forrest shrugs, tapping the bat into the orange dirt on home plate. "Marriage isn't for me, bro. I don't need to be tied down; I don't need someone nagging at me. Kids?"

He shudders, and I laugh because this is just so Forrest.

"Hey, if that's what you want, there is nothing wrong with it."

Only my two younger brothers can make me smile anymore. Their antics and opinions are just too funny not to.

"What're we talking about?" Fletch asks, winded from his jog to the middle of the park to retrieve the baseball.

"How Bowen and I are never shacking up with a wife." Forrest grabs the water bottle he set by the fence.

"Oh, why, because he can't marry Lily?" Fletch asks.

I stop, my heart ricocheting in my chest at his question. "No, who ever said that?"

"Come on, brotha. We're not fucking blind. We mighta been in middle school, but we remember the accident. We also remember how much sexual tension there is in a room with you two. Jesus, even the other day, I thought you might rip her clothes off with your teeth in the middle of Keaton's proposal."

Fletcher says all this like it's a matter of fact. And his twin nods, raising his eyebrow at me.

"And now you have to be the best man, while she's the maid of honor? Awkward much?"

"Why would it be awkward?" I ask as if I don't know just how fucking awkward this whole wedding process is going to be.

"Because weddings make people horny. Love is in the air. Bridesmaids and groomsmen do it in a closet when no one is looking. They take each other home after the after party. Everyone knows that." Fletcher shrugs, smirking.

"You're damn right, I forgot about that. Shit, Presley better have some hot bridesmaids." Forrest looks deep in thought.

"But, Lily is yours. You guys are *the* match during the wedding. The ones who will walk down the aisle right before the bride. You'll have to escort her into the reception. The best man and the maid of honor ... you'll be a pair that night."

Forrest snorts. "How the hell do you know so much about weddings?"

His twin shrugs. "Not much else to do in rehab than therapy and watch shitty chick flicks on TV."

But I don't hear their banter. Because my brothers are right ... and I'm fucking fucked. Worse than I was fucked the day before when I'd cornered Lily and had actually wanted to rip her clothes off with my teeth. Not that I'd tell them that. I would have to walk her down the aisle of the church. The church we'd talked about getting married in, once upon a time when we were naïve high school kids in love.

"It's nothing."

They both start to crack up, and Forrest steps up to the plate again. "Dude, it's not nothing. Once you get your head out of your ass and stop pretending you haven't been pining for Lily for ten years, then you'll be ready to get married."

Maybe if I hit him in the skull with this ball, he'll shut the hell up.

5
LILY

I hate the Kickoff Carnival.

It reminds me of childhood days and nights spent posing as the senator's daughter, instead of playing the kind of games where you shoot water into a clown's mouth to win a prize or riding the Tilt-a-Whirl until you puked.

My family was small, just me, my mom, and my dad ... but we were as proper and conservative as they came. My father was a Republican government official and had been in some capacity for my entire life. I was the model daughter who stood behind him next to my mother on stage; I always made good grades, wore dresses in public, volunteered, excelled at things like Girl Scouts and 4-H, and when I eventually went to college, I majored in a specialty that would bring me home again. While I loved books, and I became a librarian for me, it also didn't hurt that my father's daughter worked in a branch of the local government and gave her time furthering literacy and education.

Except for that one night, I had always been the perfect child. How my father liked to remind me of that.

The second reason I hated the Kickoff Carnival was that it reminded me of Bowen.

Everything in Fawn Hill reminded me of him ... but especially the carnival. We'd started dating almost the minute I'd walked into school as a freshman, and by the June before my first year of high school ended, my virginity was a technicality.

We'd done everything but *it*, and I was ready. We were two kids madly in love, with the heat of the summer racing through our veins. It was as feverish and lustful as teenagers could get.

And on the first night of the carnival, long after the ride lights had been turned off and all the townspeople had gone home, I gave Bowen the one gift I could never give anyone else. On a blanket he'd brought, spread on the floor of *our* gazebo, just feet from the carnival's back exit in Bloomsbury Park, we lost our virginities while whispering I love you into each other's ears.

It was so high school, so cliché. But when I look back at it, it was so sob-inducingly special that I couldn't help but shed a tear. That's how everyone's first time should be; with a person they share love and commitment with. It should be a night looked back on that warms the heart and has a glow to the memory, even if things didn't work out in the end.

So as I walk into the fair with my father, I have to literally clench all the muscles in my body. Maybe if I pretend I'm wearing armor, it won't hurt so bad.

"Senator Grantham!"

"Lily, good to see you!"

"Oh, Senator, Lily, hi!"

From all around the carnival people call out to us. This is how it is anywhere I go with my father, and I've grown accustomed to it, yet tired of it. When I'm out by myself, I get to just be Lily, the friendly librarian. That makes me sound like Spider-Man or something, but I can just be myself. I can chat about their families, or the latest restaurant I tried in Lancaster, or the movie I caught at the Cineplex.

When I'm with Senator Eric Grantham, I'm just a pretty face. Smile, nod, look up adoringly at whatever boring topic he's blabbering on and on about.

These are the times I wish I was holed up in the library, back in the shelves, organizing books and combing through old favorites. When I was there, I felt at home. Everything had a place; each story had its appropriate ending. Books were never jumbled or lost or confusing ... like the loop of thoughts playing in my head endlessly.

Books brought you to a place that helped your mind escape all the troubles reality put there.

"Lily?"

When I look up, Dad is staring expectantly at me. "Hmm?"

"Were you listening to me?"

I nod, a white lie spilling out of my mouth. "Of course."

He eyes me like he knows I'm not telling the truth. "I said I made the rounds. I don't have a speech or anything tonight, and your mother is at home waiting. I'm going to go, have a big meeting tomorrow. See you in the morning?" Dad leaned over and pressed a kiss to my hair.

Despite my annoyances with him, he's always been a good dad. Provided for me, raised me to do the right thing, and was there for all of my big moments. He might be strict, but he means well. And we might have differing political opinions—but if I told him that the world might end, so it's something I've kept to myself for nine years, since I was old enough to vote.

There are some battles that just aren't worth the trouble.

"Sounds great. I'm just going to say goodbye to Presley at her tent, and I'll walk back to my house."

"Be careful, okay? Text us when you get in." His voice is full of lecture.

"Yes, I will." I try not to roll my eyes as he leaves me in the middle of the fairway.

I'm twenty-seven years old, live in a town with five stop lights, and my parents still insist I text them when I get home to a house I bought myself. Kid gloves don't even come close to what I'm handled with.

Making sure to take the long way around, to avoid the tent where the Nash brothers and their mother, Eliza, were making caramel corn, I headed for Presley's tent.

Her yoga studio had opened just three days after the proposal at the party for friends and family, and I'd already been to two classes. Naturally, they were just as great as her classes in the park, and the space looked amazing with all its namaste vibes and natural light.

She'd been nervous to set up her own booth advertising the studio at the Summer Kickoff Carnival, but Penelope and I had convinced her it would be amazing for business.

And as I come upon the tent, I find that my best friend and I weren't wrong. Penelope had been right that people would flock to Presley's booth if they knew she was giving out free water bottles and a coupon to attend one free class. There were people flocking to my redheaded friend as she buzzed about the tent talking about yoga, health, and the need to stretch away your stress.

I smiled, waving to her as she talked, and she motioned me over. With a tilt of my head, I tried to relay that I didn't want to interrupt and I'd see her tomorrow.

Penelope was home with her three kids, and how she managed all those boys at once was beyond me. She was a warrior ... and one of the strongest, smartest people I'd ever known. Even if she tried to downplay that with her chatty blond routine.

So with both of my friends occupied, it really was time for me to head home.

The people of Fawn Hill, these people I've known all my life, smile and wave as I pass. And I suddenly feel very alone in a sea of humans who know me and my life more than anyone should know any one person. It's been put on display for them, I've been the topic of gossip for a decade now.

Yes, they mean well most of the time, but it's been hard between my father's career and my relationship going up in flames.

The noise dulls as I walk past the last ride, it's twinkling lights searing into my vision and leaving spots. I don't realize where I am until the stark white structure is in front of me, and I can't unsee it.

The gazebo.

Gosh, I wish they would raze this thing. Obviously, no one else in Fawn Hill knows the memories that exist here for me, but if I could convince someone to demolish it, I would.

Aside from the night we gave ourselves to each other, this spot was the one where Bowen took me after we saw our first movie. We would come here when neither of us could stand being in our houses, and on numerous occasions snuck here in the middle of the night just to snuggle under the stars together. It was *our* spot, and in the last ten years, I've tried as hard as I can never to come here.

But tonight, I walked into a trap. It's snagged me, a spike stabbed through my heart, pinning me right where I am.

I should turn around, but something in me whispers to my heart to walk up the three small stairs and stand inside. The minute my sandal hits the wooden planks that comprise the floor, memories assault me.

Bowen's hands in my hair. His sparkling blue eyes at twilight. Those three little words he'd whisper in my ear. The giggle fits

I'd have knowing that I'd snuck out just to meet him, and how dangerous that could be. Thinking of the risk then had sent butterflies exploding through my stomach. Our love had been wild and exciting ... with it, we could do anything.

That was exactly the reason we'd burned out in such a glorious fashion.

That was why I left the love stories to my books now. Coming up here was a mistake. I didn't need to be reminded of how badly damaged my heart was.

But before I can turn to leave, a scuffling in the dark has me jumping to attention.

And when I turn, I'm transported back in time.

6

BOWEN

My sneaker stubs the first step as I go to bolt silently, and Lily's head whips up.

Fuck, she's noticed me.

I can't very well turn around now and act like I hadn't just come to our spot to be alone. I hadn't known she was here ... hell, I hadn't seen her here since the last time she came here with me.

Did she come to our spot often?

I wouldn't admit, if asked, how many times I have found myself here over the years.

"Uh ..." Lily stutters, caught.

Even in the dark, I can tell she's blushing. It's difficult to notice when embarrassment creeps over her cheeks, because her skin is the shade of the milkiest cup of coffee. But my degree is in Lily Grantham, I studied her religiously. The slightest shade of pink will flush across the bridge of her nose, work its way down to those high cheekbones, and then settle on the edge of her jaw. I used to kiss that spot, nibble it when she'd get embarrassed around me.

"Come here often?" My voice is gruff, and I don't mean to flash the smirk looming behind my lips, but I do.

Now, Lily's eyes go wide in the dark, the white of them bugging out at me.

Her voice comes out in a whisper. "Actually, never. This is the first time I've been here since ..."

She doesn't need to say the car crash for me to know what she's thinking about.

Since I'm already here, I may as well stop teetering between the first and second step and just go all the way in.

"Were you here with your Dad?" I grit my teeth, trying to be civil and not curse at the thought of her father.

Eric Grantham and I had never liked each other much. Back then, he thought I was a cocky asshole, which I was. But I loved his daughter, I treated her like a princess, and I always put her first. Always. I wasn't one of those high school boyfriends who ignored her on the weekends or left her at parties. I always took care of her, and he knew that. He just hated that I wasn't some buttoned-up nerd with the wholesome look that furthered his senate agenda.

Everything in her father's life revolved around how much power and influence he could amass. Aside from having totally opposite views as me from a human standpoint, I just ... I could never shake the feeling that under the suit and tie, the guy was as smarmy and corrupt as the politicians you watch in movies.

When we'd almost died in the car crash, he'd used it as the perfect leverage to get me out of the picture. I'd tiptoed around him for years, trying to be on my best behavior so that he wouldn't split Lily and I up, and then I'd played right into his hand.

"Yes. Kissing babies, shaking hands." She blows out a sigh.

"So nothing has changed then?" I mean it both as a dig and an inside joke.

The fact that she's still puppeting around as the perfect daughter at twenty-seven is pathetic. But we also used to joke about this all those years ago, how fake her father could be in public.

"I don't really have much of a choice. Or much else to do with my nights. Sitting at home gets lonely," Lily admits.

We're standing on opposite sides of the gazebo, a place that holds so many immortalized nights for us.

"I know what that's like."

I shouldn't have said that. Because in this moment, she is looking at me with something akin to tenderness in her eyes, and I can't have her looking at me like that.

"Do you come here often?" Her voice is quiet.

I shouldn't have even stepped into the space at all. I've transported us back to yesteryear, and now we feel as if we have some right to visit it. I should have bolted the moment I saw her standing in here, but I was just too damn curious. What's that saying? The definition of insanity is doing the same thing over and over and expecting different results.

No matter how many times we flirted around the subject of us, the end result was that we were doomed.

But I answer her anyway. "Yes."

That one word has her rearing back, her shock palpable.

What is it about this last year that keeps pulling us together in a magnetic, forceful way? For the nine years before it, I've managed to pretty much steer clear of Lily. Yes, we live in the same town so it's inevitable that I'd bump into her at the grocery store or see a flash of her hair as she walked down the street, but the last year has put my willpower to the test.

Just like right this instant. When we're unconsciously moving toward each other, our feet moving of their own accord. Lily's eyes stay trained on mine as if I might spook. My heart rattles in my chest, the cold, dead organ shaking the dust off because it's in its matches' vicinity once more. With shaking hands, she reaches for me, in our gazebo, on a night that we spent together so many years ago.

Time has stopped, existing only between her and I. In our bubble, there is no animosity. No secrets or history or bullshit.

There is only Lily, and the love that still burns so brightly between us it could reduce this town to ashes.

That face, the one I used to kiss for hours, looms right in front of me. So I take it in my hands, and her eyes flutter shut as I touch her for the first time in a decade. My stomach twists, goose bumps cover my skin, because *my God*, I'd almost forgotten ...

How it feels to be with *her*.

"What happened to us?"

The words fall out of her mouth and detonate between us.

They rip through the walls of my heart, sending a blast to my gut, and finally, a metaphorical grenade shell to my head. I jerk back, my hand pulling away from her cheek.

Because I can't answer that question. She's asked it so many times, so many ways, and I've avoided it for so long.

If I kiss her now, I'll want to talk. Her lips on mine will unlock every secret, every emotion, I've packed away since the day my truck flipped.

And I can't do that. Not for my sake, or hers.

So, as I've done for ten whole years, I turn, walk away from her, and leave both of the organs in our chest just a little more empty.

Just a little more hollow.

7
LILY

"I mean really, there are about eight hundred styles of wedding dresses. How is any woman supposed to choose?"

Presley riffles through magazines as we sit on the living room floor of my townhouse. We have the modern bridal one, the country-themed wedding magazine, the one that has some weird, hipster vibes to it and everything in between. Our glasses are full of champagne, I've organized notebooks and fabric samples and even saved a few of my favorite floral arrangements to a folder on the photo app on my cell.

I'm going to crush this maid of honor gig.

Now that the sting of the proposal, and my Nash-less heart being wounded, has subsided, I can feel complete happiness for Presley. What's more, I'm honored she asked me to stand up for her. If wedding planning isn't the funnest thing, as well, then give me another organizational system I can dive into.

Everything from keeping track of the flowers, to talking with caterers, to alterations, to guest count ... the checklists were endless. And I loved checklists almost as much as I loved spreadsheets.

Plus, this was the exact kind of monumental planning job

that could keep my mind off the almost-kiss with Bowen the night before. Not admitting it to the girls so we can dissect every frame of last night is carving an ulcer in my stomach ... but I know that talking about it would be worse. Something is happening between Bowen and me, something that could either blossom, or more likely, bring the entire group down in flames if they were involved. I'd rather have my heart decimated quietly, alone, so that when it's time to grieve the loss of us once more, I don't have to answer to anyone.

"Ugh, just promise me you won't go with the it-style of the moment. I think I've burned most of the pictures of my wedding. The bow-sash ... the horror." Penelope cringes next to me, and we all giggle at her.

I'm glad she's part of this process, too. Who thinks, when they walk down the aisle and marry their forever man, that they'll be a widow before they're thirty? It's a fate no one should ever have to face.

But I'm glad she's smiling and joking ... even if I do know how much of a cover-up it is to mask her emotions.

"No, I'm thinking strapless mermaid, with a bit of lace. I don't work on these arms at my studio for nothing, I'm here to show these guns off on the big day." Presley makes an impressive muscle.

"You deserve it." I nod, agreeing with her. "Class the other day was like a spiritual revelation ... you're doing a great job."

Presley blushes, her pale skin unable to hide any sort of reaction to a compliment. "Thanks, mama. Honestly, I owe it all to you. If you hadn't pushed along and organized that first class in the park through the library ..."

I wave her off. "Pushing people to do what I know will make them successful is part of the job description."

She laughs and I join her. It's true though; I love my job because it's not just about books and rigid organization ...

although that side of being a librarian checks all my type A boxes. I truly do enjoy recommending reads to a person, whether it be for pleasure or, more likely, so that they can excel at something. A high school student researching for a paper, a mother who wants to learn a new dish, someone stuck in their career trying to find a new passion project ... these are all things you can use books for. Basically, what I'm trying to say, is that books are magical.

"How do you feel about pink?" Penelope asks our bride.

"The same way you feel about spring break with all three of your kids at home." Presley chuckles, taking a sip of her champagne.

Our resident mother warrior shudders. "Don't even joke about that. It's like surviving a nuclear fallout. There is cereal and poop and Legos everywhere."

I have to laugh at this because I've babysat those boys and they sure are a handful. "But at the end of the day, you have three little faces loving up at you."

Penelope nods. "That's right. I popped three humans out of my vagina for built-in love. It's not the worst plan ... honestly, most mothers would be lying if they said that wasn't an incentive of ruining said vagina."

"Good lord." I feel the blush steal over my face.

"Oh, come on, Lil ... don't act so innocent. You know you'd love some good attention south of the border." Penelope waggles her eyebrows at me.

Instantly, my whole body is scarlet. "I ... uh ..."

"When is the last time you went on a date?" Presley slaps her magazine shut, and I wish this tangent hadn't gotten us off topic.

"Not in a long time." I smile.

"But the last guy she saw for a little ... my God! He was like something out of nineteen fifties Hollywood."

Thinking of Clive, I smile. "He was a good guy, but ..."

Penelope snickers.

"What? What's so funny?" Presley whips her head back and forth between us.

"What our conservative friend isn't telling you is that gorgeous Clive had no idea how to find her clit. He couldn't locate that thing with a flashlight and a search and rescue team at his disposal."

I have to crack up at this, because sadly, for both him and I, it was true. "Oh my God ... I don't mean to be insensitive because he was so nice, but ... not even Google Maps could save that man."

"Lily! Who are you and what have you done with the senator's daughter?" Presley howls.

Penelope starts waving her finger around in the air. "I don't understand what's so difficult about it. We have a button, right at the top, full of nerves. It literally sticks out just for them to find. Some men, I swear!"

We all dissolve into a fit of snorts and a cacophony of howling laughter, and it feels so good to belly laugh that I can forget all about what almost happened last night.

Presley gets her breathing back under control after laughing so hard she's almost gasping for breath. "Back to wedding things and off the topic of everyone's coochy. I think we have the dress style nailed down, and I have a photographer I'm meeting with in Lancaster next week. I think Keaton and I have decided ... the reception has to be in Bloomsbury Park. He's adamant about getting married in the church but gave me free rein for the party. There is just too much history between us not to do it there. By the lake, that cute little gazebo, the summer sun ..."

I brush off the gazebo comment because I can't even let those thoughts filter in or I'll cry.

"Wait, the summer sun?" I eye her suspiciously.

A sheepish look steals over her expression. "So ... we're thinking we want to get married the last week of August."

"This August?" Penelope chokes on the piece of chocolate-covered caramel she just popped in her mouth.

Presley giggles. "Yes ... and don't you two look at me like I'm crazy. We just don't want to have a long engagement. It's not like we're throwing some huge soiree, it's friends and family in the park and neither of us is too hung up on the whole wedding obsession."

"What you're saying is, you don't care about wedding nonsense but are doing the traditional thing for Keaton. You're such a good wife." Penelope squeezes her hand.

And gosh, if that wasn't the most romantic thing I'd ever heard.

I slapped my hand down on the stack of magazines.

"Well, I guess our timeline was just moved up. Time to make some decisions, and fast."

8

BOWEN

My body shakes as I rip myself from sleep.

It's the only way to bring reality roaring back, the only way to remove myself from the nightmare poisoning my brain.

Even years later, I can still feel the piece of glass that embedded itself in my ribcage. About three inches down from my pec, a shard as long as a pencil and wide as a book jammed itself into my skin and missed piercing several internal organs by a fraction.

I rub the spot and can feel the raised scar where the doctor stitched me up with forty pinpricks. Not that I felt it at the time, I was so high. And the piece of glass would end up being the least damaging of any of my injuries. At the time of the crash, it was just the one I could visually see ... that shard of my truck sticking out of my abdomen. The amount of blood, although from a superficial wound, was nauseating. It was the memory I held most clearly from that night.

The one of myself hanging upside down from the driver's seat, blood pouring from my stomach.

Well, that, and looking out of the place where my windshield used to be and seeing Lily's body splashed across the pavement.

You know how they talk about adrenaline rushes and the fact that they mask any pain? I will swear to this day that's what happened. Something in me, when I saw Lily lying there, set aside all the pain in my body and put it on hold. Later, I'd learn that I had multiple breaks and fractures, plus the glass.

But at that moment, nothing else mattered but her. She'd been ejected from the car, and I'll never scrub the memory of watching her fly through the front window.

We'd been driving home after a bonfire party shortly before high school baseball playoffs. This time was my swan song, the epitome of the glory days. I had the girl I loved, a future as bright and big as the lights in Yankees stadium, school was almost over, and living was easy. I was carefree in the way only teenage superstars can be before the world smacks them down with a swift dose of reality.

I hadn't been drinking, no drugs were involved ... I'd never cared for recreational substances and I made it a point not to have a beer if Lily was in the passenger seat. I was a good boyfriend, and I wanted to keep her safe.

None of that mattered though, not when the deer jumped in front of my grill around a blind curve on a country road.

We flipped instantly, my old pickup caving in on us as the rain-slicked pavement sent my car skidding. The sound of glass crunching, the sickening thud of my head against so many surfaces, the whiplash, the burn of the airbag chemicals as they invaded my eyes.

Lily wasn't in the car for most of it. And this is where I felt the most guilty.

She'd had two beers at the fire ... enough to make her giggly and bold. I was in love with every side of her, but I knew when she got a little tipsy, she felt sexier. She'd told me as much. I'd never stop her from making her own choices, but I did want to get her home in a relatively sober state so that her father didn't try to shoot me with one of his hunting rifles.

But the alcohol had made Lily flirty and adventurous. As we drove home, her hands had roamed my lap, and I was too in love with the girl and focused on my hardening dick to tell her to stop. She unbuckled to snuggle closer, her tongue doing dirty things to my neck. We'd been young and wild, so in love that we couldn't see straight. When she went for my zipper, I groaned, tipping my head back against the seat as her warm hand had gripped me.

This is what the glory days were supposed to be like.

Two seconds later, we were spinning through the air. And when we landed, both of our lives were changed forever.

Somehow, I'd managed to get myself unbuckled, and dropped into the ceiling of my car, which was facedown on the ground. In the wreckage, I'd found Lily's cell phone, which was bashed to all hell but still miraculously, could dial.

I punched 911 in, crawled out of the window and over to Lily, dragged us into an embankment, and passed out.

I was told later, by police and doctors, that we both would have died if I wasn't able to make that call. That we would have died if I hadn't gotten us off the road, that another driver probably would have hit us coming around the blind curve.

They told me I saved her life.

Now, I wonder, at what cost? It was my fault we got into that accident. My fault I didn't anticipate, and my fault that I didn't tell Lily to sit down when she sidled up with her wandering hands.

I almost killed her, and yet she didn't stay away. Not even when she woke up from the coma she had been in for almost a month.

But by that point, I was already long gone.

By that point, the pact had been made, and I'd been sworn to secrecy.

The night of the crash haunts me in my dreams. It plagues my every waking moment and mocks the future I once had.

It's the reality I can't escape, and the other night, I almost blew the promise I made to my father.

To stay away from Lily Grantham.

9
LILY

The last thing I remember before everything goes black is the spray of a rainbow.

Even in the dark, with the rain falling in and the screech of metal on pavement, my eyes only caught on one thing.

Glass, scattering every which way, illuminated by the lights of our cell phones and the glow of the dashboard. A hundred colors, blending into one, glittering through transparent screens and sending color bouncing through my vision.

And then my head smashed into the glove compartment, and it all went blank.

They told me I was in a coma for twenty-eight days. Nearly a month. Of nothing. It's like one day I was awake and alive and well, and then I lost a chunk of time and woke back up. To me, it was as if I'd gone to sleep and twelve hours later opened my eyes. But to those around me, it was hell. Worse than hell, from those who tell the story.

Penelope had been in the Outer Banks on the night of the accident, having just gotten married at the ripe old age of twenty.

She and Travis, her deceased husband, had been on a short honeymoon before he shipped out. They'd had to come back, and she says she sat at my bedside every day for an hour.

Every single day, my family, my friends, and my doctors wondered if I'd ever wake up. Nearly twice, they'd almost lost me. I've been told that my lungs collapsed on one occasion, and on another, the bleed in my brain was so severe that I almost died on the operating table. Penelope cries when she tells that one, and I know it's the most serious thing that's ever happened in my life because my best friend does not shed a tear. Not even when *The Notebook* is on.

Miraculously, on a Tuesday in July, I woke up. It took me eight weeks to be able to speak normally again, and longer than that to finally be able to walk and run without my legs feeling like a ton of bricks.

And for all of it, my entire recovery ... Bowen was nowhere to be found.

As Penelope tells it, my boyfriend was at the hospital every single day after the accident. He would open up the place and shut it down. Visiting hours didn't apply to him, and he used to get so angry at my doctors that once they actually did throw him out.

I don't remember any of it, obviously, but my best friend says that one day, about a week before I came out of the coma, Bowen didn't show up. And then he didn't show up the next day, or the next. Penny tried to call him a couple of times, but then I woke up and everything was a flurry of emotions and testing and rehabilitation.

He was the first person I asked for when I came to. I remember that much. I also remember the sting of his absence when my mother told me Bowen hadn't been to see me in a week. How could the boy I love so much just leave me to, possibly, die? How could he not be there when I opened my eyes for the first time? Where had he gone?

I found out, about three weeks into my recovery and with a lot of cyber-sleuthing and town gossip help from Penny, that Bowen had left for technical school an hour and a half away. He'd left no letter, no voicemails ... hadn't even bothered to return the million texts I'd sent after I'd come out of the coma.

Bowen Nash had left without so much as a goodbye, and our relationship was left in limbo.

Our love had been destroyed in the car crash, and it was floating somewhere between the curve in the road, the place Bowen had swerved to avoid a deer, and the dashboard my head had slammed into. It was caught in slow-motion, unable to land, or break ... because there was no closure.

We couldn't end because Bowen had left, leaving us in this heartbreaking middle ground between sorrow and a glimmer of hope.

I wanted so badly to scream at him, to cry and stamp my foot and ask him why he left me? Still, to this day, I've never gotten the full story of the crash. Or my injuries. Or what happened to us.

Because he won't say a word. I've cornered him, written letters. I even broke down one time and asked Keaton, who just shook his head and looked at me with such pity that I spent the next two days clutching my pillow and sobbing.

Why wouldn't Bowen talk to me then, and why won't he now?

The other night, in our gazebo, was the closest I've ever come to the truth, and I wasn't even able to get a full set of questions out. He was about to kiss me; I know he was. After ten years of telling me, through silence, that he no longer loves me ... he was going to kiss me in the spot that was only ever ours.

That wasn't the action of a man who couldn't stand to look at me. Or one who had nothing to tell, nothing to feel.

I'd waited long enough. It was time for answers.

And either they were going to be the kind that would reunite us ...

Or they'd be the kind that helped me move on from the only man I'd ever loved.

10
LILY

Books have a smell impossible to duplicate.

The musk of an old story, of crisp paper and black ink. The leather scent of bindings and all the hidden traces mingled in there. The chocolate one reader swiped onto a page with her thumb because the romance novel was paired with a good box of truffles. The soda spilled onto the cover of a classic children's novel. The scent of roses or lavender candles or a delicious pot of chili ...

Yes, the stories inside were wonderful, but the scent of a physical book told so many tales too. It told the story of the reader who'd loved the journey of the characters, and what that person had been doing while they'd devoured it.

That was only part of the reason I loved spending my day among the stacks. Besides being born a bookworm, and feeling most comfortable surrounded by my favorite stories, I simply love the research aspect of my job.

Helping readers discover the book their heart is asking for, helping students find what non-fiction work would best support their essays, helping anyone decide which text was best for their project or next read ... that was my happy place.

It was like being a matchmaker, but for books. And with books, no one ever got hurt. There was always love in the end, even if there wasn't a happily ever after. Books never stopped calling, they didn't act like a jerk, and they certainly were there in all times of need.

Yeah, I'd rather spend time with my favorite characters than people any day of the week.

"Miss Grantham, can you help me find ... uhhh ..."

An adorable little girl stands before me, her blond bangs falling in front of her eyes as she tries to read the list her teacher must have handed out. She can't be more than eleven; I've gotten good at guessing ages in this job.

I smile, putting out my hand. "Here, let me see if I can't take a look."

The student looks up at me with gratitude and an innocence only afforded at that age. She's not a teenager yet, there is no hint of an attitude and the girl looks more excited to read than annoyed at her school project. I love the children at this stage, because they're genuinely happy to learn, instead of hostile when it comes to homework ... like she'll probably be in two or three years.

Looking down at the list, I realize she's supposed to pick her book for summer reading, and that's when I realize this will start happening more frequently. It's almost the last week of school, and teachers in elementary and middle school will want to talk to their students about what required reading they'll be enjoying over the summer, to carry them into the next grade.

The high schoolers have their lists and tend to read on Kindles, or worse, just watch the movie.

But I love helping the fifth and sixth graders most. Because they're excited about the books, and they have a little bit of freedom. They get to choose which two books they'll read, from a list of some of my favorites.

"Hmm, well, what kind of books do you like to read?" I ask her.

I know which books on this list I'd recommend, but I never want to sway someone walking into my library. While I want young readers to branch out, I also want them to continue reading and enjoy it. Taking their favorite books into account will only further their love for them and will provide the basis to make them lifelong story feasters.

She bites her lip and looks down, one shoelace untied. "Well ... I liked *A Wrinkle in Time*. And *Tuck Everlasting*. But my favorite is *Harry Potter* ... my mom and I are reading the first book together at night."

Hmm, so she likes fantasy. Some magic, some sci-fi ... and *Tuck Everlasting* has some romance in there. But overall, this little lady has some great taste.

I walk around the counter and crouch to her level so that she trusts my judgment more.

"Those are all great reads. *Harry Potter* is one of my favorites, too. Based on your epic list of books already read, I'd go with *The Giver* and *Chronicles of Narnia*. Those are two of my favorites ... you can't go wrong with those books."

I give her a little conspiratorial wink and write down the aisle numbers for her, and she's off, skipping along to find her next story.

"You're going to be a wonderful mother someday,"

a familiar voice says from behind me as I stand and watch the girl disappear between the shelves.

I turn to see my own mother, standing on the other side of the counter, smiling at me.

"Mom." A grin splits my face as I walk into her arms for a hug.

Out of all the people in my life, my mom is my favorite. A breast cancer survivor two times over, she's strong and resilient.

My mother is the silent, supportive wife to a loud, outspoken politician, and while she may play a role in front of the cameras, she is the real head of our family. She is tough but fair, lovely and elegant, and has a way of being on your side without painting the world in rose-colored shades. When I got into fights with friends or had my heart broken or cursed a teacher for giving me a grade I felt I didn't deserve, she would always hug me and give me a shoulder to cry on. But then we'd have an earnest conversation about the other side of the argument, and by the end of our talk, I'd see things in a different light.

My mother is the person who shaped who I am today, and I'm glad she is the female figure I get to look up to.

"If I learned anything about dealing with children, it's from you." I squeeze her once more before pulling back.

We're a matched set, my mom and I. Same long dark hair, same blue eyes, same miniature stature.

"Well, whenever you're ready, I'm here to watch them." Her ocean-colored pools search mine.

I roll my eyes. "I think a lot of things would need to happen before children. Say, a boyfriend, perhaps."

Chuckling, my mom walks to the cart stacked high with books I need to re-shelve. "I don't think that's the problem, my dear. There are a hundred men who'd fall all over themselves to land an intelligent, kind, beautiful woman like you. The thing is, you only want one."

So that's why she's here. Is this the "go after him again" talk or the "you need to move on talk"? I wish I could gauge her mood, but she's got her nose buried in the front flap of the latest romance novel that just arrived in the library.

A few minutes go by, and I move to the computer, checking on orders and emails. Mom sighs, picking up another book and closing it forcefully. She wants me to look at her.

"What is it, Mother?" Frustration itches my scalp.

"Love isn't easy, Lily. I thought I taught you that by this point."

"Mom, seriously? We've had this conversation a million times. It's been ten years. The man does not want me."

She tucks a lock from her signature bob haircut behind her ear. "Oh, nonsense, darling. Do you think I'd still be here if I took no for an answer? Not just with your father, but on this earth. I love that man, but your daddy has done some reprehensible things. I almost shot him when he voted against that public education bill ... you might not remember it because you were little but he slept on the couch for a month. And if I'd let cancer tell me it wanted to take my whole body, well, I'd be dead. You have to fight for the things you want. Nothing is ever going to come easy."

"I have fought, Mama. You know I have. He won't listen or talk, so I'm out of options."

Mom shakes her head again. "One last time. You have to try one last time. I know he dropped you off at your apartment. And someone saw you together at the carnival."

"Seriously, people in this town have got to get lives of their own." I blow a frustrated huff through my nose as I struggle to keep my composure.

"That might be. But ... that intel leads me to believe you two are talking again. Or at least, seeing each other."

"I don't know, Mom." I finally relent, not wanting to be badgered about Bowen anymore.

She lifts her hands in surrender when she's the one who came to pick the fight. "All right, all right. I'm just saying ... that looks like an opening to me."

Her arms wrap around me once more before she walks out of my library, and I wonder if she just came in here to rile me up. Probably. Mothers didn't exist if they weren't stirring the pot most of the time.

I hated to admit that her little pep talk had given me a reason to act.

Then again, I'd never disobeyed an order from my parents. And this was, by all means, an order.

I was both aggravated with my mother, for interfering and using the cancer card on me. But I was also re-energized about talking to Bowen. About getting the answers I deserved.

And gosh darn if that wasn't her plan all along.

11

BOWEN

"Oh, come on, guys ... can we just have a night where no one gets punched or arrested," Keaton whines as Gerry sets two shot glasses down in front of Forrest and me. It's our second round of Johnny Walker, and if my rich little brother was buying, I wasn't saying no.

I'd had a hell of a week, what with the increased nightmares, two fire calls I'd been present for, and the whopping quarterly taxes on the shop I'd had to pay ... fuck yes I was ready for some stupid decisions.

"Who says this is going to get out of hand?" Forrest snickers as he sputters from the poison sliding down his throat.

Because when my brothers and I got together, trouble always followed. There were four of us; big, egotistical males all cocky and daring in our own ways ... there was bound to be shenanigans.

Obviously, Fletcher wasn't with us tonight. He'd bowed out of nights at the Goat & Barrister since getting out of rehab, which was a decision I respected and was happy he made on his own. He seemed to be making good choices these days, and I hoped he stayed on this path.

"Come on, big bro, drink up." Forrest sets a shot each in front of us.

"Ah, what the hell." Keaton shrugs, slamming it back.

"That's a change of attitude if I ever saw one." I cough as the alcohol burns my nostrils.

"Presley is on her way over, and she wanted us to have a 'fun, drunk night' as she puts it. Says we're getting too boring and married. Have to keep my woman happy."

Forrest laughs. "While that makes me want to cringe, I think it's hilarious she called you boring. Maybe she really does see the real you."

"You invited the girls?" The annoyance in my tone is not hidden.

Or lost on them. Keaton rolls his eyes. "Lighten up, Bowen. They're all in the wedding party, and she's my fiancée. There are plenty of other people in this bar, you don't have to talk to Lily if you don't want to."

The door at the front of the bar creaks with an arrival, and speak of the devil, Presley, Lily, and Penelope all walk in.

And Christ, if she doesn't look fucking hot.

Lily never knows how truly seductive she is, and that's part of the appeal. In tight jean shorts that fray at the edges, a pretty blue tank dotted with flowers, and those summer wedge sandals that make a woman's legs look impossibly long ... fuck I want to do so many inappropriate things to her.

My dick begins to harden in my jeans because the alcohol is loosening my inhibitions and damn it if that long, curling brown hair wouldn't look perfect tangled in my fingers.

Shut up, cock. I can't let myself anywhere near her, or I'll definitely do something stupid tonight.

"Ladies," Forrest greets them, his eyes lingering too long on

Penelope.

Presley saunters over to Keaton, kissing him noisily. Lily stands off to the side, waves at my brothers, and then walks off farther down the bar to ask Gerry for a drink.

"Dream on, little Nash." Penelope flicks her long blond mane over her shoulder, and her very generous breasts shift in her white sundress.

Forrest places an elbow on the bar. "Let me buy you a drink and we can talk about those dreams I have."

I snort because the pickup line is terrible. My little brother has always had a hard-on for Penelope, ever since he saw her in a bikini at the local pool when he was twelve.

Of course, she was eighteen and completely in love with Travis. Honestly, even now that he's gone, Forrest stands no chance. Penelope would chew him up and spit him out.

"You're so obnoxious." She rolls her eyes. "But I'll take a white wine spritzer."

Or, maybe he does stand a chance. Crazier things have happened.

With those two bickering on one side and Keaton and Presley practically humping each other on the other side of me, I glance around for something else to do.

The dart board is empty, and no one is picking a song at the jukebox right now. But, because she's in the room, my eyes only ever stray to her. Like magnets, we're always locked in to each other's energy.

Before I can tell myself what a bad idea this is, I'm walking over to Lily. So much for staying away from her. I'm going to blame the alcohol and ignore the voice telling me I've been waiting for a moment like this for years.

For a moment where I can scapegoat my low inhibitions just to get close to her.

A small smile splits my lips as I scoot onto the stool next to hers. "Always nursing that one lone gin and tonic."

Lily blinks as she looks up and sees me, her cheeks pinking up. "It's my drink of choice. Tried wine for a while, but it gave me a headache. Then I tried vodka, and after just one ended up ..."

She shudders and I know that's the liquor that had her puking. Everyone has *that one* liquor. Mine is bourbon. I shudder even thinking that right now.

"But, when I tried this at one of the galas my father was speaking at, I liked it. It's what I've stuck, too. I'm not much for change, the regular old tried and true is good for me."

"I remember." I chuckle, the damn beer and whiskey doing the talking. "I like that about you."

She looks stunned, and those big blue eyes flick to my mouth. God, how I wish I could lean over and kiss her. Or better yet ...

"What are you drinking?" She points to my glass, her fingernail a pale pink.

And wasn't that just a damn tease. Because now I was imagining a whole fist of pink nails wrapped around my cock. That was just so Lily. A tiger wrapped in a lamb's disguise. I knew what she sounded like when she came. I was the first man who'd ever touched her, who'd ever shown her how to wrap her fist around ...

"Bowen?" The way she says my name, I know I've been sitting here staring at her like a damn fool.

Fuck, I needed to get it together. "It's uh, whiskey. But, there has been a hell of a lot of things mixed in there tonight."

She chuckles. "Big guy's night out, huh?"

"Something like that." I smile back.

We stare at each other for a minute, and I can feel both of our heads moving closer. Almost unconsciously, as if there is a string tethering our mouths together.

"Are you having fun?" She breathes.

"More now than I was before." It's the truth.

Lily's eyes dilate. "Why is that?"

"I think you know why."

How easy it is to fall back into this. A decade has passed without a word. And now ... we've been sliding slowly down this hill of attraction since my brother's engagement. It's slippery and dangerous, and I'm always grappling to climb my way back up. But sitting here with her, the woman I love most in the world, it's too good to stop. I may break when I eventually hit the ground, but if it means staring at her, speaking words I've kept locked up in my heart for ten years, then so be it.

"Maybe ..." Lily sighs, breaking the moment. "Listen, we're going to be around each other a lot more now. With Presley and Keaton getting married, there will be more nights than there were in the last ten years where we'll probably run into each other. You clearly don't want to talk about us ... and I can't understand that, but I do know that I can't keep cutting myself down over it. Even if we're not friends, maybe we can just ... be cordial. I don't hate you, Bowen. Not even a little. And you've said as much about me. Maybe we can ..."

She is going to say, be friends. But we can't. And she has no idea why. Here she is, trying to appeal to my softer side, trying to bridge a gap that I've caused. God, Lily is the best kind of person. Even when someone has repeatedly cut her down, she'll still try to shake their hand and call it a truce.

It's a good thing, for both of us, that I'm the worst kind of person.

Because I was teetering on the edge of doing something disastrously stupid, something that could damage both of our reputations. I was willing to break just to have one moment of *us*. But now, I have to break *for* her, to protect her.

"No. We aren't friends, Lily. We've never been friends. Just because we have to be in the same rooms doesn't mean we need to talk. Or even look at each other."

The look in her eyes ... it's as if I've slapped her. So much shame and hurt cloud those baby blues, and I feel the knife twisting deeper into the ventricles of my heart.

"God, when is enough going to be enough?" I slam the rest of my whiskey back, psyching myself up to destroy the love of the most amazing woman in the world. "Don't you get it? This is desperate and sad. We were over a long time ago. I don't want you. What is going to make you understand that?"

In the middle of my total annihilation of her, her phone buzzes. She picks it up, using anything to escape from this attack.

"It's my parents. They want to make sure I got home, say it's too late."

I snort, the alcohol making me especially mean tonight. "Wouldn't want to disappoint the senator and his wife. Oh, wait, I shouldn't use the word disappoint. The word is disobey."

Lily's eyes grow cold, and that's good. It's what I want. "You're despicable."

"And you're weak. You've never had one thought for yourself. One thought that wasn't put there by them."

This asshole comment has a different effect. Her entire face fills with upset, and I'm sure she's about to crumble.

"I have to go." A single tear falls.

"Yeah, go do whatever mommy and daddy tell you to. It's what you do best."

Lily sends me one last defeated, humiliated, heartbroken look as she grabs her purse and bolts from the bar.

My own soul may be cracked in half, but my mission is accomplished.

Hopefully, I've done enough damage that she'll stay away, and never discover the secret that divides us.

12
BOWEN

The collar on the tux was pulling so tight, I couldn't seem to get a good breath in.

"I feel like some Vegas showboy," I grumble.

Keaton laughs at my uncomfortableness. "Presley doesn't care what we wear, but I've always envisioned a tux when I'm standing at that altar."

"Of course, you have, why would you dream of anything else? Old-fashioned, stiff, conservative ... wait are we talking about you or the tux?" I smirk.

He huffs in annoyance but can't move to sucker punch me in the arm because the tailor has pins dangerously close to his junk.

When he asked me to come with him to get fitted for the wedding, I guess I didn't realize I'd be wearing a suit, too. Or, more accurately, a tuxedo. The thing was stuffy and restricting, but I wasn't complaining as much as I could because I was supposed to be the best man.

I'd been poked and prodded all morning, but at least it was almost over. And at least I had Keaton alone.

Because I needed to talk to someone. Me, the guy who never

wanted to form words, couldn't help but wanting to spew the thoughts spinning around in my head.

After last night, after almost slipping up and kissing Lily for the second time in as many weeks, I needed a game plan.

Without a doubt, I felt rotten, like I'd poisoned myself, thinking about the things I'd said to her. They were fucking horrible. But I'd needed to do something to get her away from me. These chance meetings, the moments in private, they were becoming a regular thing. It had to stop. I wasn't strong enough to resist her much longer.

Being in her presence, it hurts too much. I was so blindly in love with this girl from the moment she crossed my path, she basically concussed me. There was no explanation to it either; one second, there was the world before her, and the next, everything shifted. What we had, still have, is that inexplicable kind of love. The kind that defies logic and years, that keeps burning brightly no matter how much you try to extinguish it.

She was around too much now. Those long brown curls, her eyes the color of a midnight sky filled with stars, that perfume that haunted my dreams ... Lily was breaking me down and she didn't even know it. But for her sake, and mine, I had to poison her against me.

Once I'd slept off the depression of slicing her with my words, and the massive alcohol hangover, I'd started plotting.

The one thing that had brought me joy, besides Lily, and still did ... that was baseball. After my college prospects dried up, I was bitter and didn't want anything to do with the sport. I could have gone into a program for sports broadcasting, with all of my knowledge. I could have gone to school to be a gym teacher, and went the coach route, eventually. Hell, I had enough contacts and inroads that I could have done something.

But I'd been young and angry, and I'd said screw you to the

sport that no longer wanted me for the way I wanted to exist within it.

Truth was, it had been ten years, but I still kept in touch with a few of my contacts from back then. I was friendly with some of the assistants and scouts, and it got me thinking …

"I've uh … been thinking about giving Lewis Mider a call." I start the conversation, already feeling like the suit had shrunk three sizes with how uncomfortable my skin felt.

Keaton's eyebrows go up. "The scout who was recruiting you for UNC?"

"You've got a good memory, brother." I nod. "Yeah. We've exchanged a few emails over the years, and I was thinking I might see if he has a position. Or knows of anyone in the industry who's hiring."

"To be a scout?" Keaton frowns.

"Or a coach. Or … anything." I shrug.

Keaton slips out of the suit jacket and slings it over the back of a folding chair. "What's this all about, Bow?"

I'm not good at talking about feelings. Scratch that, I'm fucking terrible at it, and I rarely ever do it. But something has been itching me, picking at me like a kid at a scab, ever since Keaton and Presley got engaged.

For the last ten years, I've let life happen to me. I let my baseball career vanish because I couldn't play as well. I let Dad convince me that the barbershop would be a good investment once the old owner put it up for sale. I haven't dated, haven't let go of the anger, haven't … anything.

I'm not one to wish for rainbows and sunshine, far from it actually, but maybe getting out of Fawn Hill could give me the fresh start I've needed since I flipped my truck that night.

"I miss baseball. And I need something … else. Maybe if I leave town, I can find it."

There, that was opening up.

Keaton snorts. "Well, that was about as detailed as I thought it would be."

I glare at him.

He holds his hands up. "But it was better than usual, I'll give you that. If this is what you want ... if it will make you happy, then I say go for it. You'd be an awesome coach, or scout, or whatever. We both know that baseball is your first love. I just ... I want to make sure you're doing this for the right reasons."

"And what are the wrong reasons?" I bristle.

"The wrong reason would be doing this to run away from your problems. The easy solution is moving out of town, leaving all of the turmoil behind. The hard thing ... would be talking to her."

Now it's the death stare that I shoot back at him. "You know I can't do that."

Keaton's eyes are sad, and he gives a slow nod.

I don't let him get a word in. "Plus, I've been sitting in the same place for ten years. This wouldn't be running. This would be breaking free. From the things that have held me down for a decade. I might not be able to play, but I can be around the sport. I don't know ... something about you and Presley, Keat. It eats at me. What the hell am I doing? I have a dead-end life."

"I don't view it that way. You have a successful business, you fight fires to help and save people, you have your family."

His words don't even puncture the surface. "You know what I mean. The life I have ... it's a fallback avenue. I've never been anywhere but here; I have no experience or miles on me. I'm almost thirty years old, single, living in the town I grew up in with no ... motivation. Nothing is a challenge."

Keaton smiles, looks down shaking his head. "Damn, you just described my life before I met Presley. And ... I can admit that I felt many of the same feelings. But, then I found love."

I can't look at him now. "I had that, once. And it's gone, it has to be dead and you know why. At least I can try to find a way back to a part of the person I once was."

Keaton is silent for a long time, long enough that the tailor comes back and marks both of our pants and tells us we can change and meet at the register.

Finally, he clears his throat. "You should call him. If this is the way you're going to break down that wall you've surrounded yourself with, and trapped yourself inside of, then I think you should call him."

13

LILY

Three days after the total dismantling of my self-esteem thanks to Bowen, all I want to do is sit in my house and lick my wounds.

Too bad it's dress shopping day.

"Yippee," I sarcastically recite as Penelope pulls into the parking lot of the only wedding and bridesmaid dress store in fifty miles. Of course, I want to see another woman in a wedding dress today. Of course, I want to try on whatever horrible creation they've invented to make bridesmaids feel even more like bridesmaids. Of course, I want to toast with champagne and celebrate love.

Lord, I should have taken something for this.

I'm never the type to be grouchy. It literally goes against my chemical makeup, and I can recount on one hand the total number of times I've ever been outwardly mean or prickly in my life. But today, it would have to be the first finger on the second hand.

Something shifted in me after Bowen took me down a notch. Okay ... it was probably more like twenty notches.

For a man to go from almost kissing you, for the second time in a month, to completely slaughtering your confidence, love for him, and values you hold dear ... it was—and I never curse—a mindfuck. I didn't know which way was up. When Bowen had started going in on my, what he called, desperation and weakness, it was worse than our breakup.

Because when our relationship ended, I didn't get words. It was radio silence. But to hear him voice those opinions about me, to pull apart every fiber of myself that I thought was worth something ... it hurt like hell. To tell me he didn't love me, that he didn't even want to look at me ...

I have to bite my tongue to keep from crying in the backseat of Penelope's car, next to one of her kid's car seats. There were two gummy bears smashed into the lining, and I had to focus on that to stop myself from losing it.

But nothing stung as bad as hearing Bowen call me weak in regard to my parents. He knew me better than anyone, even after ten years of barely speaking, and he knew that was the touchiest subject for me. Because ... I was weak when it came to them.

Bowen had been there for all the phone calls telling me to get home now. He'd been there through campaign speeches and caucus trips and the smiling and waving. All the things I was forced to do that I didn't want to because it fell under "being a good political daughter." Each party, or dance, or night with friends that I missed because I was out doing something for my dad's position or campaign.

He had been the one I'd cried to, complained to. Back then, he'd stood up for me, privately between the two of us. And now, it seemed he was using all the ammo he'd amassed against me.

It was cruel. Each word that had shot like venom out of his mouth and at me was so incredibly cruel.

Penelope and Presley have already gotten out of the car, and I'm lagging a few seconds behind as I drag myself onto the pavement.

"Earth to Lily, where you at?" Penelope snaps in my face.

I swat her hand away. "I'm here."

"Woah, who are you and where is Lily? We're shopping for fluffy white dresses ... looking at wedding gowns is one of your favorite pastimes." Penelope eyes me like an alien has taken over my body.

"I'm fine. This is Presley's day, don't worry about me." I try to smile but it feels so forced that my cheeks hurt.

Presley seems to be too absorbed in the excitement of the day to latch onto my sour mood. "Ah, I didn't think I'd be this nervous when we got here. I mean, I don't even really care about wedding stuff, just the whole marrying Keaton part matters in my mind. But ... this is my fashion moment. I only get to do this once."

Penelope nods. "That's right, so make it count. You can have whichever one you want. Mostly because Keaton is paying."

Presley bumps her hip. "Who says Dr. Do-Good is paying? I own my own business, thank you very much."

"How is the studio doing?" I ask, happy to talk about anything unrelated to weddings or love.

"It's doing amazing, actually. There was a write-up about it in the Lancaster newspaper, which is so cool. And our memberships have steadily been growing. I mean, it's only the first month, but we're making money. I was able to squirrel away some for Grandma because she refuses to take a salary. I just ... I can't believe I get to go to work every day and teach yoga."

I nod, knowing exactly how that felt. "Do what you love and you'll never work a day in your life."

"Always quoting." Presley chuckles. "Such a librarian thing."

I shrug. "Books are the best medicine. Which is why I prescribe them every day."

Penelope makes a gagging noise. "Yuck, kill me with the sappiness. We're shopping for wedding dresses; this is already as

Hallmark movie as it gets. At least entertain me with some dick stories."

My teeth grind together. Most days, I love my best friend. Today, however, with her raunchy comments and annoying over-enthusiasm, and my terrible mood, I want to strangle her.

But, Presley indulges her. "Is it true that sex gets better after marriage?"

"Most people would say the opposite, but my sex life was amazing. Although, inconsistent, what with the husband overseas in a war zone." Penelope shrugs, and it's the first time I've heard her talk about Travis in a while.

Which is strange. She never mentions him, not even to me.

"Well, I think ours is going to get better. Not that it's not amazing now, but since the engagement ... hell ..." A blush flushes across Presley's cheeks, and the color almost matches her hair. "When was the last time you had sex?"

Penelope and I look at each other, and my best friend points at me. "I'm thinking that question was aimed at you."

My grouchiness crowds in. "That's not really your business. How about you tell us when you last had sex, Penelope?"

I lash out and say this to hurt her because I know she hasn't been with anyone since Travis died two years ago. But instead of snapping back at me, her eyes shift nervously and she scurries for the door of the bridal boutique.

What the hell? "Um, Penelope, answer the question."

Presley goes after her too, her eyes curious. "Did you sleep with someone?"

"Welcome, ladies." A store employee walks up on us at that exact moment, and I giggle without thinking about clamping my mouth shut.

She definitely heard us asking Penelope if she'd had sex with someone.

"Hi, I'm Presley McDaniel, I made an appointment for all of us to try on dresses for my wedding today."

The woman checks the book at the front counter. "Yes, we have a dressing room waiting for you. Come on back."

I grab Penelope's elbow as Presley walks in front of us. "What is going on? You met someone?"

My best friend sighs. "I didn't meet anyone, Little Miss Priss. I fucked someone."

"*Penelope!*" I whisper scold.

She rolls her eyes. "What? There is a huge difference. Don't go making a big deal out of things. I just ... it was time, and the moment was hot. So I did it. There are no wedding bells or happily ever afters in my future."

That made me sad for her. And for me. We'd been stuck in the same boat for a while now, and I was worried for her. Setting aside my own failed love life, Penelope deserved someone to care for her. She and Travis had been soul mates, but it didn't mean there wasn't someone out there for her to spend time with.

A frown turns my lips down all the way through the first two dress try-ons. Presley and Penelope are bubbly and vivacious, sipping on champagne and dancing around in tulle. I try to be supportive, give my thoughts on the dresses, but with each change, I sink further into the gloom drowning me.

I shouldn't have come here today.

Walking out of the small dressing room the attendant hung my bridesmaid dress options in, I glance at myself in the mirror. It's pale pink and floor length, with lace detail from the bust to the shoulders and a low scooping back.

The material is airy and light, and the way its small train is dragging ...

A tear falls accidentally before I can scoop it up or blink it away.

"Are you crying?" Penelope walks out in a blue tea length dress and rushes over.

I sniffle, covering my face. "No, just allergies."

"You're crying?" Presley comes out now, in a long-sleeve lace gown that she looks gorgeous in.

Another tear falls, because now they're on either side of me, holding my shoulders. And I can't help but breakdown now that they're near, now that someone is comforting me. I wish they would have ignored me, so I wasn't sitting in a wedding dress shop sobbing.

"Is this why you've been surly all morning?" Presley hugs me, her voice gentle.

Forming a sentence right now would be difficult, so I just cry as she holds me, and Penelope rubs my back. Once I'm close to settling down, when the sobs are nothing but intermittent hiccups, Penelope tips my face up to look into hers.

"Can you tell us what's wrong now?"

I shrug, looking at the bottom of the dress as it drapes onto the floor. "Bowen and I ... we talked when we all went out to the Goat. He said some pretty awful things, but the gist of it was that he's no longer interested in me, thinks I'm desperate and weak and doesn't want to have to look at me when we're at the same functions."

"He said that? That motherfucker, I'll cut his balls off!" Penelope yells in a fit of rage.

Presley is quiet, hanging back in her opinion to see if I need to say anything else. I don't, because saying that felt like taking a bullet. I didn't need to speak again.

"That wasn't very nice of him. And I'm on your side, he's an idiot and an asshole for it. But I think something else is going on with Bowen."

"Yeah, he's a prick, that's what's going on. You don't need to deal with his bullshit any longer, Lil." Penelope hugs me.

My eyes connect with Presley, and while I want to give Bowen the benefit of the doubt, I've done that for too long. It's time to see him for what he truly is. And that's a guy who isn't worth my love or time.

"I'm sorry to break down on your day." I hope she can read how apologetic the look in my eyes is.

She pats my arm. "Don't apologize. You needed to let it out. Do you feel better?"

I took a second to search my soul, and I had to admit, I felt lighter after having a breakdown all over my friends. "Actually, I kind of do."

Presley claps her hands. "Good, because I think I found my dress!"

14

BOWEN

In the end, I email Lewis Mider, who is now a scout for one of the local triple-A teams.

He responds within two days and is happy to hear from me. And while he knows his organization isn't looking for anyone right now, he may have a lead with a team in Ohio and will keep me posted.

Just reading that email sets something loose in my chest. I'm not sure if I'm happy about his response, scared of what it may bring, nervous about possibly leaving the town I've always lived in ...

It's probably all the above, but I'm too superstitious to even talk about it. And if that isn't a baseball player mentality, I don't know what is.

But I do open up the barbershop feeling much lighter than I have in weeks.

And that's when he walks in.

There is nothing outwardly intimidating about his body language, or even his stature. No, on the contrary, Senator Eric Grantham isn't a particularly large or burly man. He has a willowy build, is shorter than I am, and has a head full of half-gray hair.

But it's the way the man carries himself. His presence demands respects, reeks of power and a nose turned up in every direction. I've never liked the man, not even when I openly loved his daughter.

And he's never hidden the fact that he hates me. On sight, I knew from the first moment he saw me that he didn't think I was good enough for his daughter. Hell, I thought that a majority of the time, still do, but that was her decision to make.

"Bowen, my boy, thought I'd come in for a nice, fresh cut before I head down to Philadelphia." The way he calls me boy is so condescending that my hands curl into fists.

No one else is in the shop, it's a Wednesday and too early for even the morning birds to arrive. This was strategic, and something in my gut tells me he is not just here for a haircut.

But what am I going to do? It will be worse if I turn him out. The man has more power than anyone in Fawn Hill, and I don't need to be even further down on his shit list.

He crosses the room to where I motion for him to sit at my station because I can't seem to make words come out of my mouth. Lily's father has had the same high and tight buzz since he got out of the military years before I was even born, and I could do that cut in my sleep.

Even so, he holds up a hand before I pick up my razor. "Don't cut me and keep it even on the sides."

My teeth grind together as I try not to take my clippers to his eyeball. *Prick*. First, he walks into my shop to try to intimidate me, and now he's telling me how to do my job?

I start buzzing, the sound drowning out the silence as I try not to rush to get him the fuck out of here.

"So, Bowen, how's life?" The smug bastard grins at me like we're old pals.

"It's good," I say tightly.

He nods, and I have to anticipate the movement of his head so as not to fuck up the cut. Grantham knows this, too, because he smirks. He's challenging me on purpose.

"Some people have been talking ... saying you've been seen around town with my daughter?"

Fuck. So that's why he came in here, to see if I'm honoring my end of the deal. Not only does he want to throw his weight around, but he's trying to warn me off.

It's more condescending that he can't just call her Lily. As if I have no association with her, as if we don't know each other.

"We both live in Fawn Hill. My brother is marrying her friend. It's inevitable that I'd see her."

"But are you trying to *see* her?" His voice is sharp, direct.

Does he want me to confess I'm trying to fuck his daughter or something? What the hell does this prick want? Besides ruining my life more than he already has.

"I've been trying to avoid Lily since the moment my father told me to. Or don't you already know that? I'm sticking to your little pact, Senator. Even if my father is six feet under." My words are biting, and I switch the guard on the razor to fade the sides of his hair.

I may be the one with the electric blade in my hands, but I feel weak. Powerless. The man sitting in my chair has this invisible hold over me, his upper hand in this situation is so clear that we both sense it. He knows that he's calling the shots, even if I have a semi-weapon moving over his scalp.

"I'm glad to hear you picked up your father's end of things when he died. Perhaps you're a smarter boy than I thought you were."

Notice how he calls me a boy and not a man.

I finish his hair, a sour pride rising in my chest because even if this asshole was subtly threatening me the entire cut, I did a damn good job.

My mind travels back to the day my father sat me down. It was about a month and a half after the accident, my arm was still in a sling with pins holding my wrist together. Those were the hopeful days, the ones where we still thought there was a chance I'd get full functionality back. A chance that I'd make it to the majors like all the scouts who'd come to see me play said I would.

Dad had asked me to join him at the kitchen table, and I hadn't thought it was strange back then that not one of our four other family members were in the house. He'd asked me how I was feeling, if the pain had gotten any better, and told me he was so happy that I was here and healthy.

But then ... the father that I knew came out. I loved my dad, fiercely, and still to this day think he was a great man. But he also had his flaws. His need to appear as a pillar of the community sometimes overshadowed the *right* thing in the situation. He wanted to protect his boys, but not at the expense of becoming a social pariah.

I know now why he did what he did. My father struck a deal with the devil to protect our family, and to protect me. My life was headed in the direction of baseball greatness, that's what I'd told him I always wanted most. And he'd tried to preserve that for me.

But in the process, he'd promised Eric Grantham that I would stay away from his daughter. Lily's father had hated me on sight, and it had been years of enduring his under-the-breath comments whenever I picked her up or spent time at their home. The state senator had power in places that a family like mine couldn't even fathom. At the time, I hadn't realized that. I'd thought my father was just forbidding me to see the girl I was in love with because he thought we were bad for each other, and she'd ruin my future.

Now I knew it was twofold. From the snippets of information I'd been able to bleed out of my father over the seven years before he died, but after the accident, I'd learned that both he and Eric agreed that Lily and I were better off not being together. Our love blinded us ... which back then, was probably true.

However, it also encouraged us to be better people. We supported each other to follow our dreams and love that unconditional wasn't easily found. I wish my father had seen that ... because he had it with my mother.

Both my father and Eric had threatened mutually assured destruction. If I didn't stay away from Lily, the state senator would use his influence to make sure my father's business and reputation were ruined. And, although I don't know if he ever had this kind of leverage, he promised my father he could ruin my chances of getting recruited by a division one university.

My father, in turn, threatened to reveal the truth about who caused the accident. Rumors were more deadly than power, sometimes, and spreading one to the town of Fawn Hill that innocent Lily Grantham had unbuckled and had her hands down her boyfriend's pants at the time of the crash ... that would ruin the political shine of her family.

Even now, my father's words burn in my gut. I wanted to hit him so badly back then, and even though he's six feet under now, I could still sink a nice uppercut and feel no guilt. It was a shameful, fucking awful thing he did. He looked at it as protecting his family, keeping his son's ambitions intact.

I saw, and still see, it as the biggest sabotage of my life. He left that secret on me, told me the details of their horrible agreement, while Lily never got a hint of what went down. And that's my secret to keep. I will never tell her the disgusting words her father said about her, or how he continued to control her life even when we thought she might not make it.

Our eyes connect in the mirror. "Don't worry, I've ruined my relationship with Lily to the point of no return. Just like you have, if she ever finds out what you did."

I can't resist getting that jab in, because he's a twisted bastard.

The senator's face goes scarlet with anger. "I'm warning you, boy, I can do a lot more damage to you now than I could have done then. This shop, your home, your mother—"

"Don't you dare bring my mother into this, you piece of shit!" That gets my blood boiling.

He smirks, having gotten me to lose my temper. "Careful, Bowen, you wouldn't want to do anything to make me mad. Plus, if Lily ever found out, which she won't or there will be hell to pay, what's stopping me from pinning the whole secret on you? She has no idea what happened back then. You wouldn't want my daughter to think you left her because let's say, she was a danger to your baseball career. That you didn't visit her in the hospital because you were angry that she made you drive that truck off the road."

Lies. It's all fucking lies. And he knows it, but Lily doesn't. He could say whatever he wants to her, twist the truth until it resembled nothing like the pact our fathers made. Until he convinced her I'd been the bad guy behind it all. After all, I had barely spoken to her in ten years, and he was her trusted and loving father.

I fucking hated him. "Get out of my shop."

"Do you understand what I'm saying, boy?" He grins, an evil expression clouding his features.

"Get. Out. Of. My. Shop," I grit out, ready to spit nails and sucker punch him if he says one more thing.

He must sense my temper about to teeter over the edge because he gets up and walks out. Without even paying me.

As he gets to the door, he pulls out his wallet, throwing a ten-dollar bill on the floor. "Glad we came to that agreement. Until next time, Bowen."

It takes me a full three hours until my heart rate is normal enough to take the "out to lunch" sign off the door. The prick wound me up so much that I had to run home over lunch.

Not to eat. But to beat the shit out of the punching bag in my basement.

15

LILY

Two weeks pass with no major blips on the wedding planning front and no disastrous run-ins with Bowen.

I go to work, clean my house, read a few good books, help Presley prepare centerpieces, babysit Penelope's boys twice while she goes out of town for a sales conference, and accompany my parents on a trip to Philadelphia for an event my father is a part of.

Mom and I walk the streets of the city while Dad shakes hands and makes appearances, and I'm so happy to take a break from Fawn Hill that I'm smiling more than I have in two months.

"You look good, dear." Mom pats my hand as we walk, holding it in hers.

"I feel good," I say, smiling at her.

The city bustles with energy, and although it exhausts me by the end of the day because I am a small-town girl through and through, the change of pace is nice. All the commotion helps drown out thoughts you don't want to deal with, and it's a much-needed break from my spiral of worrying.

"Thank you for coming on the trip." She squeezes my hand and then lets go.

In my other hand, I clutch two big shopping bags. One from the Amish market, and another from an art gallery we stumbled upon. There were two prints of lilies, and I couldn't not buy them to frame and hang somewhere in my house. They were too perfect.

"Not as if I had a choice." I give her a half-joking smile.

"You always have a choice." Mom frowns at me.

She says this as if we both don't know how this goes. From the time I could say political campaign, I'd been included in one. I'd never consented to being paraded around in the dresses or bows, I smiled for all the cameras, trained with interview coaches and was even scolded by a couple of campaign workers about my report card grades when I'd brought home a B plus in middle school.

"This could tarnish your father's reputation."

That's what it always boiled down to. I lived a life walking on eggshells, worrying about how every move I made would reflect on my father.

For twenty-seven years, I'd played along. But recently, maybe over the past year or two, it had all grown very old. Not that I'd ever disclose this to my parents, but I tended to side with the party my father wasn't affiliated to. And what's worse, what they would disown me over ... I didn't even really care about politics. It was all a bunch of stuffy old men in suits arguing about where money should go.

Yes, I'm aware there is more to it than that, but government has just never been my cup of tea. I'd rather help people on a ground level, face-to-face, with as much kindness as I can. That's why I am a librarian. My sole job is to help others find joy or information from inside the pages of books.

What my father does? It's all a facade. One I'd grown very tired of.

And my mother putting on this act like she isn't a cog in the wheel ... it's frustrating.

"Mom, I love you, but don't bullshit me."

"Lily! Language." Mother looks around as if the political correctness police could pop out from any random sewer grate.

"I'm serious. Dad practically packed my bag for me. I had to get Madison to cover at the library for me on such short notice, we'd ended up having to cancel two of the kid's reading circles we'd had planned for the week."

"Surely, they won't mind rescheduling those." She shrugs as if it's an afterthought.

"They might not, but I do. I have a job, I run a library. I mind when I have to move things around, not only because it creates scheduling nightmares, but because it means I'm breaking my word. All because I'm a grown woman who has to take mandatory trips with her senator father!"

Mom sighs and I take a breath, surprised at my sudden outburst.

She takes a seat on a bench as we come to the Schuylkill River Trail, and pats beside her, signaling for me to sit down.

"Sweetheart ... I'm sorry. From day one, you've been our pride and joy. And we only ever wanted to take you everywhere with us. I know you've grown up being watched, in the press at times, and made to feel like everything you do is judged."

Her breath catches, and when I look over, she's pressing a hand to her chest.

"Oh, Mom ..." And now I feel bad, because I've made her feel like a jerk. "I didn't mean ... I grew up with a wonderful childhood, a wonderful life ..."

And I meant that. I'd always had everything I'd ever wanted or wished for. They'd been great supporters and my parents had always told me they loved me.

She waves me off. "Just listen, okay? Maybe your father and I didn't take into account how much this world can affect a child. We were young and naïve when he got elected, we didn't know anyone else in government. We were just trying to live the life we thought would give you and the citizens of Pennsylvania the best future. We're your parents, but we're also just people, Lily. People are flawed. They make mistakes. Just because we raised you doesn't mean we were always right."

It's humbling to hear her admit that.

"Your father ... I think he demands you be here because he's proud to show you all he's accomplished. You drive him, motivate him to work harder. But if you really don't want to be a part of this public life, of this government family life, then tell your father. He will understand, I know he will."

She said it with such confidence, I almost thought it was true. And while I believed that Mom thought Dad would respond well to this talk, I had my doubts.

Five hours later, and we're well into the second course of dinner at a charity event honoring the cancer institute in the city.

The event is honoring many small-town politicians, from state senators to local assemblyman to mayors, who have helped raise funds and passed bills for the institute. It's a wonderful cause, and I'm especially grateful to attend this event because there are actual pediatric survivors in attendance. Each of the survivors and their families are being given a week's stay in a vacation location of their choice.

While it might be my preference that they open college funds for each of them, lord knows there is money to go around, it is nice that these families who have been through so much get to spend some quality time relaxing together.

I've spent much of the night talking to the children, who are easily the most interesting and intelligent people here. I'm not kidding either ... half of my father's colleagues are blowhards going on about their privilege in unironic ways, and the other half are just trying to get a better look down my dress. They skeeve me out, and I realize that I should really stop coming to these.

My knife is halfway through my roast duck when Dad speaks up.

"Lily, I have someone I want you to meet," he says casually from the other side of Mom, who sits between us.

We're surrounded by other Pennsylvania politicians, and no one is really paying attention to us. But I know ... this isn't a request. And it's not a setup.

He needs something.

How do I know this? Because he's done it before. Introduced me to some junior politician who will probably think I'm pretty and listen to me about my father's policies. The first time he did it, I hadn't even realized I'd just been prostituted out for politics.

Not that I ever had to leave the ballroom with them, or even accept a drink. But my father thought by having his attractive daughter, in her form-fitting dress, talk about his views rather than the old man doing it himself ... he thought it garnered more support. That if I batted my eyelashes and smiled, it would win him an ally.

I'd done this five or six times before I started to object. It was weird and dirty ... it made me feel cheap. And the fact that my own father devised this strategy ... I felt like just another pawn on his political chessboard.

"I'm eating, and I don't feel like meeting anyone new," I say quietly, trying not to have the other members of our table overhear.

I hear his fork clatter as he tries to set it down calmly. "You really should meet this junior senator from New Jersey. You two could discuss many things."

This isn't a suggestion, and both my mother and I know it. She looks up at her husband, her eyes suspicious.

"If she says she doesn't want to meet him, she doesn't have to meet him." Her tone is chastising.

My father gives me a look that could translate to daggers being thrown. "But I know that they would have a very good conversation."

Now my bones are on edge, and my leg bounces up and down under the table. "And I said *no*."

"I don't know why you're making such a big deal out of this, Lily." My father sighs, exasperated.

He doesn't get why I'm making a big deal? I want to scream at him. This is the side of him that I loathe, the one I downright hate. The pompous Senator Grantham, the man who thinks he can walk all over people and tell them what to do with his nose high up in the clouds.

This man, the jerk sitting on the other side of my mother, has taken over the doting father that I still see from time to time.

This is not the parent who would kiss my scraped knees and tell me to get back up and play. I missed that part of my father, the one who'd take me for ice cream before dinner without telling Mom. Or drive really fast over the train tracks because he knew I liked how my stomach dropped out in that quick burst of air the car got off the jump.

And now I understand why Bowen made those comments. The alcohol that night only fueled him to speak more harshly about my father than he ever has before. But he was right. More and more, I saw this ... almost *evil* side of my father. Something had happened to him over the years, and it would be easy to say he changed after the accident, but the truth was, it had been a slow corruption of his soul. With more frequent trips to Washington, more responsibility as he became a senior senator, and the amount of power he'd amassed ... my father had become someone I didn't like all that much.

He'd become someone who, frankly, I was beginning to hate.

I take my napkin off of my lap, dabbing my lips and then setting it on my plate, which is only a third eaten.

"If you'll excuse me, I'm going to call it a night."

My mother startles beside me. "What?"

Her voice is a whisper-hiss because she doesn't want to draw more attention to this argument.

"Sit back down." My father's voice, however, is laced with irate authority.

Scooting my chair back, I smooth my dress before standing. "I hope you two enjoy the rest of the night. I'll be taking a car back to Fawn Hill, *tonight.*"

It might be juvenile, and I may look like a spoiled brat, but the defiance fills my chest with confidence. I've *very rarely* said no to my parents, but I'm beginning to reach the end of my patience. They still treat me like a five-year-old, and this is my life I get to live. I want to tell them that I will no longer be attending events, speeches, or rallies, but we both know that isn't true. Plus, having that temper tantrum here in public would be even more embarrassing than leaving in the middle of dinner already is.

Not that I care what the people sitting around us think.

"You're making a big mistake, Lily." My father's eyes are flinty as he glares at me.

But as I walk out of the ballroom, I feel like I've just made the first decision concerning my happiness in a very long time.

16

BOWEN

I keep thinking about those first moments with Lily.

Ever since her father came into my shop and basically threatened to ruin my life if I didn't stay away from her, I couldn't stop thinking about those early days. It was like his visit had brought on memories of how much he'd disliked me even from the start, and those could only be accompanied by how brand-new our relationship had been.

Back in those days, we had been shiny. Untarnished. I remember the first time we hung out outside of school. Like the typical cocky, sophomore jock that I was, I'd sauntered up to her at the end of ninth period in the cafeteria and invited her to an upper-class party that one of the seniors was throwing that Friday. When she'd showed up with her friends, innocent little freshman, I'd stolen her away with two red cups of beer and a devilish smile.

We'd spent the whole night on the back porch, flirting. Well, more like me trying to get to know her, and Lily answering shyly as she gulped down her beer for confidence and stared at her feet.

Halfway through the conversation, I'd interrupted in the

middle of her telling me which book she was reading and kissed her. Planted one right on her. When I pulled back, my lips and fingers and spine tingling with some indescribable gut feeling, Lily was stunned ...

"Why did you do that?" she'd asked.

"Because you're nervous. And I'm nervous. And I wanted to get that out of the way because I plan on doing it a lot more. But first I want to know everything about you," I'd said.

"That was my first kiss." She'd blinked.

"Good," I'd said. *"I want to be your only."*

Jesus Christ, I'd been a cocky little shit. But I hadn't been lying. Lily and I, we were love at first sight. Once we'd locked eyes, there was no way to stop it from happening.

"Four-alarm ..."

HISS, crackle, a beat of silence.

"Explosion, all units respond ..."

Radio static, crackle ... hiss ...

Toothpaste coats the bowl of my sink from where I just spit, and I turn the faucet on to wash it away and rinse my brush. I got lost in my thoughts of Lily in between my bedtime routine and missed something on the police scanner I keep by my bed. But it keeps cutting in and out, and something sounds fishy.

Did I hear the word explosion?

Walking through the hall of my second floor, I turn into my bedroom, where the police radio sits on the corner of my desk. The piece of furniture is against the wall across from my bed, a king-sized monster which was the only splurge purchase I made when I bought my house.

Two years ago, I'd finally saved enough money and could afford a mortgage without defaulting on my business. The barbershop was making good money, and I'd decided to invest in Fawn Hill. Not that the small Pennsylvania town had a booming real estate market with out-of-towners vying for a plot of land, but this was my home and I knew I would stay here forever, so I might as well live in a place where I didn't have to share a wall with loud neighbors, or worse, my brothers.

Just as I'm about to turn the radio up to listen closely, my phone rings on the nightstand beside my bed.

Quickly, I move for it, grabbing it as I see Keith's, the town fire chief, name flash across the screen.

"Keith, what's going on?" I'm already up, pulling a pair of basketball shorts on over my boxers.

"Bowen, sorry to call you in like this, but I need you here now. You know that suspected meth house out past the county line?"

Did I know it? Without a doubt, I did. I'd dragged my brother out of that place half-alive not less than a year ago.

But I don't say as much. "Yeah, I know the place."

On the other end of the phone, it sounds like the sky is falling down. "Damn fools went and got themselves blown up. The fire is bad, at least a four-alarm, and it's spreading to the trees. We need to contain it before it gets to the surrounding farms. We need all the hands we can get."

"I'll be there in twenty." I'm nodding, knowing the drive takes thirty-five.

The phone goes dead before I can end the call abruptly. I run to my closet, shuck off the basketball shorts and dig in the back to find the spare set of fire pants I keep here. I grab for my boots, pull my protective socks on and then shove my feet into the bulky pair of shoes. I'll find a jacket and the rest of my gear when I get there.

I just need to get there.

As promised, I'm at the scene of the fire in twenty minutes flat. I did almost eighty all the way here, and if I hadn't slammed the detachable siren to the top of my truck, I would have been pulled over for sure. Not that every cop in a fifty-mile radius wasn't on site at this blaze.

"Keith!" I run up, waving frantically to the chief.

"Bowen, thank God you're here. The rest of the guys need some relief, plus we think there are still two vics trapped inside."

I could argue that these guys really weren't victims, but I didn't know the semantics of who was in that house, and there wasn't time for hostility.

"Grab your gear and grab a hose." He pats me hard on the back and I'm off.

Into the truck, grab my jacket, helmet, gloves ... race back out, check the lines on the truck, see who needs the most help.

My eyes assess every inch of the situation, from the way the flames lick up from the foundation of the house to the roof and fly up toward the canopy of trees above. The smell of acrid flesh and soot hangs in the air, and it's either horrible that I'm used to it or a relief to know that I'm no longer affected by the scent of burning skin. All around me, organized chaos ensues, and I pinpoint where I'm needed most.

I know Keith told me to help man the tree line, to keep the fire from spreading past the forest and to the land beyond ... but that's never been my strong suit. Part of why I'm an asset on our all-volunteer team is because I'm quick. Maybe not quick enough to run the bases professionally, but I'm fast, especially for my brawny size.

I need to go into that house.

My boots clomp toward the porch, the wood there all but crumbling as men try to douse the flames long enough to bolt through the front door.

Being a firefighter, or any emergency responder means fighting every single instinct to run that invades your brain. While others are running away from danger, you're running toward it. While buildings are falling, you're marching into them to help save anyone you can grab. It's against all logic to do this, yet in some twisted corner of my brain, there is a thrill extracted from it. Maybe I'm tempting fate, taunting death ... but besides wanting to save lives and help people, I do this because I'm ill in some sort of way.

"Keith, give me the okay to go in." I stare him down.

He assesses me, looks at the house, and then back to my helmeted face again. Keith always has a level head, even under the most stressful situations. Measuring what takes priority is why he has the job that he does, and that also comes with picking the right person, with the right skill set, for the job.

Me? I am fast, and I can carry fifty pounds more than a lot of these guys. I can jump higher, and for some reason, the smoke has never affected me as much. I don't have a wife or children ... essentially, if I'm lost in a fire, no one will miss me. These are things a good chief or captain will weigh out.

And clearly, Keith does. "Go! Go! But if you feel that floor going out, or that building start to come down, get the hell out. You don't need to be the ultimate hero, not at this scene."

What he's saying is, these guys got themselves into this mess, and he doesn't want me killing myself over them.

In an instant, I'm running into the building, ash and fire raining down on me. The front door is a ring of flames and I push past it, the heat trapping itself inside my suit. I can feel the sweat slicking every part of my body and feel the way my lungs begin to seize. This is the thick of it ... this is what I dread but also what I crave.

There is coughing coming from the next room, and I'm surprised anyone is still conscious at this point. With smoke this thick, I won't even really be able to see anyone, I just have to go on instinct.

As I walk, the floorboards under my boots are literally melting. I feel the give of them with my weight. It's the human equivalent of walking on eggshells. In front of me, I feel something move, and I bend, reaching out with my gloves. A hand fumbles for me, and I can't even see a face, but I immediately crouch, trying to scoop whoever this is up.

And then the world commences to crumble around me, flames swallowing my body whole.

The last thing I see is a vision of Lily, her arms extended toward me, mouthing the words *I love you*.

17

LILY

From somewhere within the darkness of my bedroom, something buzzes.

I flip over, burying my head beneath the covers and throwing my leg over the enormous body pillow I sleep with. It's probably a text from a friend out at the Goat right now, having a drink. Or maybe it's an update from Facebook or one of my news apps. Either way, I'd made a plan to come to bed early tonight, and I was wiped.

In about three minutes, I'd be snoring into my white ruffled sheets.

The phone vibrates again, and I sigh. I'm on the verge of that dreamy peacefulness, that point where you're right on the edge of sleep and nothing has ever felt so relaxing. But my cell has knocked me out of that alternate state of reality, and now I'm staring up at the ceiling in the darkness, debating whether I should pick the darn thing up.

I know if I do, the light will pierce my eyes, and I'll have to shield them. I'll end up bopping all over social media, and in another hour, I'll glance at the clock and chastise myself for even giving in to the addictive piece of technology in the first place.

Weak, that's what I am. Because I scoot over in bed, reaching for my nightstand, and turn my phone over. When I do, I squint at the screen.

Three text messages from Presley. *Hmm, that's odd.*

Not because we don't text all the time, but we don't ever really talk at night. She usually reserves that time for Keaton and has never been much of a technology girl since I've met her. Her nose isn't permanently pressed to the screen like the rest of us.

Punching in my password, I flick my thumb over the messages app and open them up to read.

Presley: *Hey, do you hear those sirens?*

Presley: *Oh, never mind, Keaton just got a call from Bowen. There has been a fire on the outskirts of town. They think it might be the meth house.*

Her texts are about ten minutes apart, and now that I really strain my ears, I can hear the sirens blaring somewhere in the distance. A fire ... at the meth house. The one they saved Fletcher from almost a year ago, I remember the story. The local police had been trying to nab those guys for months, and now it looked like they'd gone and done their job for them.

I shouldn't think like that, but those men were evil. I'd heard about what they'd said to Presley, what they'd done to Fletcher. Who knows how many more poor souls they'd enticed and trapped with their drugs? It was a morally corrupt business they were into, and any karma that came their way was deserved.

Even so, I sent a quick prayer up for everyone at the scene, for them to be safe from the fire.

Lily: *Have you heard anything else? How bad is it? Is anyone hurt?*

Sitting up, my foot begins to jiggle. The nervous energy travels all the way up my body, and into my hands, which shake slightly where I hold the phone. I click out of the message and scroll through some social media feeds, just biding time and trying not to worry. Presley isn't answering, and I'm not sure why, but some sixth sense tells me something is wrong.

It takes Presley another forty minutes to answer me, and by that point, all the lights in my bedroom are on and I'm pacing.

Presley: *There was an explosion, Bowen got called in to help. The house collapsed, not sure who was inside. That's everything I know. Try to update you as my news comes in.*

Dread swamps me, sending a cold sweat slicking down my back. I wasn't with Bowen when he trained to be a firefighter, but it doesn't mean I didn't know he was doing it. While I find it admirable, and honestly, ridiculously hot ... I also hate it. Fawn Hill and its surrounding towns don't have much of a crime or fire rate, but it doesn't mean that both jobs still aren't dangerous. The description of the career is literally putting your life on the line anytime they need it, and right now, he was running into a burning building. The thought of losing him, the man I'd loved my entire adult life, even more than I already had ...

Fear is a virus spreading through my limbs as I pull on clothes, ready for what, I'm not sure. Do I assume at this moment that I'll go drive out to the fire, try to get to him? I'm not thinking rationally, that much is clear. But I can't help it. Even if he doesn't want me, even after the hurtful things he said that night at the bar, even if the two of us mean nothing to each other ... I can't bear not to be there if he's hurt.

My phone dings again, and I dive for it.

Presley: *Keaton is trying to find out as much as he can. Word is, the fire has spread to the surrounding forest. They're trying their best to put it out.*

I can't sit here, alone, while Bowen might be dying on the outskirts of town. That is what my brain in haywire chaos tells me, and before I know what I'm doing, my keys are in my hand and I'm walking out the front door. It's only nine o'clock, but it feels like the darkness is closing in on me as I walk cautiously through my neighborhood. In reality, most of the people here are probably still awake, and I'm just letting the ghosts in my head spook me more than I should.

The distance between my townhouse and Bowen's craftsman is nothing ... and it doesn't escape me on my nightly drive home from the library that we're basically neighbors even though he hadn't known that until recently. For over a year, we've lived down the street, in the same town, and couldn't bring ourselves to speak about the past.

Now here I was, standing on his front porch, ringing the bell. What a stupid thing to do ... clearly, he wasn't home. Presley had told me as much, and the house was dark with his truck missing out of the driveway. But it's instinct, and I'm surprisingly disappointed when I'm not greeted by that annoyed, gorgeous face opening the door.

I stand there, indecisive, sure that I should walk home but my feet won't move.

I'll just ... sit here until I see his truck turn down the street and then I can go. I just need the reassurance he's okay, and he won't know I was ever here.

So I sit down on the top porch step and lean my head against the white wood railing. I don't even realize when I drift off, the summer night wind breezing through my hair.

"Lily?" A gruff, surprised tone invades my ear, and I blink my eyes open.

My vision is hazy and at first, I think I'm in a dream ... until the smell of the man standing in front of me hits my nose.

I blink again, straightening up where I sit on his front porch and look around me.

"I ... I must have fallen asleep." The fog of my unexpected nap still shrouds me. "You're okay."

He nods, tilting his head in confusion at my being here. "Did you ... how are you ..."

Bowen trails off, not really knowing what question to ask, and I take a moment to study him. His hair is wild, brushed this way and that ... but still sexy in its chaos. His face is streaked with soot and dirt and sweat ... and is that blood? His uniform pants are almost black, the greenish-yellow of them completely covered. The blue of his eyes is dulled, and he looks exhausted. The way his bones sag shows just how much he's been through tonight.

I look up into his face, not moving from where I sit on the steps. "Presley texted me ... about the fire. Said you were in the house. I ..."

Swallow the emotion, Lily. I gulp, telling myself that I cannot cry in front of him. It would be foolish and misplaced, and he doesn't care for me. Not the way I care for him.

"You were worried about me?" More questions.

"Of course, I was." My voice cracks.

Bowen leans on the railing of his porch, the scent of him reminding me of the danger he just escaped. "I've never seen anything like it. There were casualties, but all of our men got out okay. I'm okay. You didn't need to come here. I don't need you to take care of me, haven't I said that? Now, go home."

And just like that, I'm dismissed. Bowen Nash has no time for me or the feelings that will never leave my heart. It crushes me, my soul literally dropping to its knees. If I'd lost him tonight, not that he was mine to lose, but if he'd ...

I don't know how I could go on living in a world that he wasn't a part of, no matter how much he didn't love me back now.

Rising from his porch, I walk off of it, my head hung low with shame.

Bowen doesn't thank me, or say good night, or even pat me on the back for coming to make sure he was okay. And that angers me. So much so that a few angry drops graze my cheeks on their way down.

Thank God I'm already on the sidewalk, in the dark, where he can't see me cry.

But the question on the tip of my tongue won't let me leave. I whip around, squaring my shoulders.

"If I were the one in the burning building, would you even save me?"

I say this to his back, his body already halfway to his own front door. The massive figure of brawn and grace stops, the muscles on his back under his T-shirt rippling with tension.

When Bowen turns, his eyes are feral. "What did you say?"

"You heard me," I spit back. "I came here, worried out of my mind, to see if you were alive, and you can't even bother to look at me. If I was gone, would you even notice?"

The last sentence out of my mouth is so raw, so honest, that it burns all the way up my throat. Because that's the thought I've been wondering all these years. If I disappeared tomorrow, would he even care?

I feel him before I see him, that's how fast he moves. Like a panther catching its prey, one minute Bowen is on the porch, and the next, he's grabbing me, hoisting me up by the waist.

And crushing his mouth to mine.

Complete shock. Sensory overload. A million memories and

a thrilling new secret that is heady and lustful and so many other emotions I can't process.

The man I have loved for my entire life is kissing me for the first time in ten years, and it takes me a second to realize I need to take this opportunity to kiss him back.

To pour every ounce of pain and admiration I've harbored for the last decade into this display of love.

Because even if this all ends in a few minutes, even if he puts me down, lets me go, pretends this never happened ...

I can make it through another ten years knowing that we had this. Even if I don't understand it. Or whether Bowen is doing this out of spite or because he hurts as much as I do.

Right here. Right now. We have this.

18

LILY

"Bow—" I pull back, my lips grazing his, but he doesn't let me speak.

The way he pulls my mouth back to his, forcefully, with the hand that isn't looped around my waist and holding me up ... it's possessive. My body is his, it always has been, and he knows it. With one flick of his tongue, he undoes me. Bowen unwinds the barbed wire that has held my heart hostage for ten years. The lock he placed on it springs open.

In the middle of the sidewalk, at God knows what hour of the night, here we stand. Two star-crossed lovers, the man holding the woman up as she clings to him, not able to get close enough to each other as they express wordlessly all that has come between them.

His mouth is hot and unrelenting. We're making love with our lips, tongues, and teeth. The kisses are sharp, direct, but also fumbling and unpracticed.

Bowen's body is hard and rough beneath my fingertips, beneath the legs wrapped around his waist. He's grown from a boy into a man in the time we've been apart, and my hands ache to touch all of that bare muscle.

Our mouths still fused; he carries me in long strides to the house. Up the front porch, in through the front door where he wrenches his key in the lock, and into the foyer.

I've never been here and can't tear my attention away from our kisses to take a look at the place Bowen calls home. Maybe at another time, I'd be curious to see how his house is set up. I'd want to digest every detail, right down to the floorboards. Right this moment, it doesn't matter.

Bowen sets me down, his lips leaving my mouth and trailing down to my jaw. I can barely breathe I'm so turned on. God, how long has it been since I felt this kind of desire? The kind that had me embarrassingly slick in my underwear, moaning loudly into the air with just the contact of his lips on my neck.

Ten years. It has been ten years.

He walks us backward, pulling his soiled shirt off and throwing it somewhere behind us. Muscles, farther than the eye can see, chord from his neck to his happy trail. He's got more than a smattering of hair now, to demonstrate just how much he's grown up. Dark, and thicker as it descends, I know that he'll be all male below that belt. Bowen is rugged, a little dirty, and it's making me grow wetter by the second.

I'm entranced, my eyes closing of their own volition, as Bowen continues to suck and lick at my neck as his large fingers reach for the hem of my shirt. In an instant, it's gone, and then so are the bike shorts I pulled on in a frenzy to get over here.

Only when my back hits a wall do I gasp, reality creeping in. I'm half-naked in Bowen Nash's entryway.

The door to reality is slammed quickly closed though, when I hear the pop of the buttons on his pants, and glance down to watch him drag the zipper open.

"The last thing I thought, as the house collapsed around me, was that I'd never see you again."

My head snaps up. Those ocean blue eyes, the color of the eye of a storm, pierce me. I'm wordless, dissolving into him.

"For ten years, I've felt ... empty. Destroyed. I am not me without you. And I was going to burn up in that house without ever telling you that."

Bowen braces himself against the wall, looming over me, his free hand pulling my wisp of a bralette up and over my head. My hands go to his hips, pushing the rough fabric of his pants down and over them. I know the moment his cock springs free because I feel the weight of it on my arm, but our eyes are still locked on each other.

I tingle everywhere, my skin is on fire. Prickly, hot, uncomfortable, sensational ... all rolled into one. I want him inside of me so badly that I could cry right now.

But what's pulling at every ventricle of the muscle in my chest, are his words. Because I too am destroyed. I too am empty.

"Fill me up," I whisper.

It's an invitation, but it's also a plea. Fill my heart, fill my soul. Use your body to make me whole again.

A low growl emits from Bowen's throat. He wrenches my plain gray boy shorts down, and I step out of them. I'm completely naked, standing in front of him. He steps back a fraction, those blue eyes turning to melting icebergs as they trace the lines of my body.

I take my time too, staring at the Adonis who's just toed out of his fire boots and kicked his jeans and boxers across the room. He's so much bigger ... everywhere. I gulp, need swamping me like the best kind of humidity. It sticks to my skin and sends a trickle of sweat down my spine. My eyes lower to the impressive cock bobbing between us, and I have to rub my thighs together to alleviate the friction zipping between my legs.

Bowen moves swiftly, picking me up again and smashing his mouth to mine. God, *yes*. I've been a woman on the verge of dying from thirst, and now I'm drowning. He maneuvers me until my back is pushed up against the wall and his arms are locked under my knees. I'm spread impossibly wide for him, spread eagle against his foyer wall, and some other time I might blush about this, but I'm so aroused that I can't care.

My arms loop around his neck, my right hand burying in his hair and latching on. He hisses as I tug a little, but the pain sends a flash of heat through his eyes.

"The life you would have with me ... it's not one you'd want. There are ... things you don't know, Lily. Things you'd hate me for."

"How many times do you have to nearly die for it to get through? I have no life without you," I whisper, searching his eyes as tears pool in mine.

And that's when he pushes into me, so painfully good that I moan low in my throat.

Bowen pins me, holds me open for him as he impales me over and over again. Nothing about this is gentle or slow, and I love it. We're frenzied, having ten years of pent up sexual tension and heartbreak will do that to two people.

With each stroke, each grunt, each loll of my head onto his shoulder, the chokehold on my heart eases.

"Lily ..." Bowen's voice is a plea.

I'm so close, my clit rubbing against the rough hair at the base of his cock. Every time he seats himself fully inside of me, I shudder with the sharp stab of pleasure/pain.

"Bowen." I could say his name forever if he promises never to let this end.

I don't want to think about what happens when this ends.

He picks up speed if that's even possible because he was already jackhammering into me with precision. But now he's practically making a dent in the wall with my body, and I may bruise tomorrow but right now it feels so exquisite that I don't care.

"Don't stop. Never stop," I chant, my words meant to be about way more than just sex.

Bowen's lips close around a nipple, pulling the peak with his teeth, and I'm gone.

My thighs tighten in his big hands, and the sensations take over my body. They rob me of all five senses, and I ride the climax greedily. I haven't felt this euphoric in a decade.

My forehead meets Bowen's shoulder, and just as my orgasm begins to subside, he sets it off again as he comes with a loud growl that rips through the silence of the night.

He's like a wild animal, calling his mate with a sound only meant for her ears. It has me choking on words I can't say.

So instead, I hang on, my arms tightening after we're done.

I'm not ready to let go again.

19

BOWEN

In the moment before I'd kissed her, I knew it was a terrible idea.

I should have never turned around, never run off my front porch, never slammed my mouth down on hers and broken the thread holding my resolve together.

Because now that it was broken, there was no going back.

I'd tasted her, had said things that were now branded onto my heart. I'd looked into her eyes as she came undone and it was like watching my whole purpose come into focus.

Everything made sense when I was with Lily. I had been put on this earth, in Fawn Hill, to fall in love with her.

Less than a month ago, her father had walked into my barbershop and threatened my livelihood and my family if I went anywhere near her. The thought had flitted through my head as I was stomping toward her on the sidewalk, but the bottom had already fallen out. I was already tumbling, unable to stop what was inevitably about to happen.

Last night was a blur. We started in the hallway, smashed against the wall opposite my front door, and didn't stop until my bed sheets were ripped halfway off the mattress and our bodies were too weak to keep going.

As I blink open my eyes, the harsh sunlight illuminating the reality of what just happened, I survey the damage.

"It looks like a bomb went off in here." Lily sighs as she turns over, her thin arm draping across my abs.

"You read my mind." I swallow the lump in my throat, both from sleep and emotion.

"I guess that's what happens after ten years of waiting." She chuckles.

Her eyes are still closed, those long dark lashes fanning over her sun-kissed cheeks. Long locks of chocolate-colored hair curl over my pillows, and besides the smile gracing her lips, she wears nothing else.

I can't help the hands that smooth up and down her back and the thigh thrown over my leg. Last night in the entryway was a bad idea. So was bringing her upstairs. So was the third time I pushed inside of her, around four a.m.

And now here we are, waking up together in my bed, pretending like we don't have a mountain of issues to sort through.

Even with all of that sitting on my shoulders, my needy dick still stiffens as she trails her fingers over my stomach.

"Hey, none of that." I squirm when she hits a ticklish spot.

"I forgot how ticklish you are." She proves this point by moving her devilish fingers up to my armpits.

The sensation is annoying, and to stop her, I flip over onto her and pin her arms. The minute her playful expression beams up at me, our situation slaps me right back down to earth.

The accident. Her father. The secret I'm keeping. The fact that I love her but can't act on it.

I roll off of Lily and right out of bed, picking up my boxers as

I head for the bathroom. I don't bother to shut the door, and as I take a piss, shout out into the bedroom.

"This was fun, but I have stuff to do today. So I'll uh, see you around."

It's cold and callous, and it feels like a rusty blade thrusts through my heart as I say it. But I have to get her out of here. I've already compromised myself too much, and if I go back to that bed, there is a chance I'll never leave.

I walk back out, averting my eyes from the bed where Lily still sits. Rifling through my drawers, I pick out a T-shirt and pair of shorts.

"Don't do this." Her voice sounds so small.

I slam a drawer shut. "No, don't *you* do this. It's not a big thing."

"It's the biggest thing. This is monumental, so stop acting like I'm some chick you brought home to fuck and throw out."

The curse word coming off her lips twists my gut. Indeed, what just happened is huge. Of course, she's not just some chick.

"I don't know why you still blame yourself for that night," she whispers.

Anger, hot and shameful, rages through my veins. And I snap. "You were in a coma for almost a month, Lily! I almost killed you. How the hell do you think I'm not going to blame myself for that?"

I turn, throwing my arms up and screaming at her.

Tears streak her bronzed cheekbones. "You weren't drinking, Bowen. You had a seatbelt on ... it was my own decision to take mine off. We were stupid, we were kids. The road was slick, and the deer jumped out in front of us. That isn't your fault, it never has been. I'll never forgive myself for how reckless I was. But I can't forgive myself even more if you think that you caused that accident. Because it's just not true."

So I guess we're going there.

"You can't know that."

"All I know is, I woke up from a coma having lost so much, in such pain with weeks of therapy ahead of me, and the person I loved the most wouldn't even speak to me. You didn't even come to see me in the hospital." The sob she chokes out is the worst sound I've ever heard.

It shatters my already dead heart, but her last sentence puts flint in my eyes. "I came to visit you *every single day*. I left my hospital bed, unplugged myself from the machines when they told me not to, limped across the halls to get to you. I held your hand as much as they would possibly let me. I prayed to God that you would wake up, and we both know I am not religious. Lily, I was there every day. Until—"

My voice cuts off, maybe out of the need to preserve what little I have left. I was dangerously close to revealing the truth, something she can never find out.

"Until what?" Lily looks at me, those deep blue eyes pleading.

I stay silent, and she gets so fed up she actually gets up, walks over, and pushes me in the chest. "Until what, Bowen? Why won't you ever just really talk to me?"

But, I can't. If she knew what ... what our fathers had done ... I could never ruin her world that way. It was better to cut both of our hearts out than put her through that.

So I don't answer.

My feet prepare to move, to pick up her clothes and toss them on the bed, to shrug into my own shirt.

In the harsh light of day, my mistake doesn't look like love. It looks like damnation.

"No." Her voice is sharp.

I turn to see this beautiful creature, naked and standing in the middle of my room, the morning light falling across her gorgeous body in luminescent stripes. All that caramel skin, bare breasts, it's distracting when I should have a stiff upper lip right now.

"No, what?" I growl, my cock hardening.

"I'm not leaving. Not until we talk. I'm not taking no for an answer this time. And it'll cause a *whole lot of gossip* in this town if you toss me outside naked right now. So you have no choice."

She's manhandling me. And I don't like to be told what to do. "Get out."

"No." Lily gets right up in my face, confronting the beast without a shred of fear in her eyes.

"Lily ..." I warn.

"I'm not afraid of you," she challenges.

She should be. About the secret I hold.

I advance on her, putting my arms on her waist to give her a nudge out the door. But all that does is fuck me over big time. Because she's still naked, and damn it does she feel amazing.

"Let's go downstairs. We'll have breakfast. I'll cook. And we'll talk." Her suggestion is quiet, a peace offering.

And because my hands are on her bare hips, and I'm a glutton for punishment, I agree.

"Fine. But we're having sausage, not bacon."

"Typical." Lily shakes her head as she smiles.

20

LILY

Standing in a kitchen, barefoot in sweats after a night of sleeping in the same bed as Bowen Nash.

My sixteen-year-old self is living out her biggest fantasy right now.

I was totally that girl who doodled Mrs. Lily Nash in her notebooks and listened to sappy teen love songs while imagining a time when Bowen and I could live together without curfews or adult supervision.

It's oddly familiar now that we're actually doing it. As if we haven't missed a beat of the last ten years.

"Put more cheese in those," I tell Bowen.

"There are already six slices in here, and we're only making six eggs to split. That's way too cheesy."

I scoff. "There is no such thing as too much cheese. Put more in."

"Bossy," Bowen says under his breath, scrambling the eggs and adding more cheese. "Do you still prefer tea over coffee?"

He moves to the pot he put on before but opens the cabinet to reveal a box looking suspiciously like my favorite kind of green tea.

"You drink that brand of Twinings?"

Bowen shrugs, but I don't miss the flash of a blush, as if he's caught, that steals over his face. "It's not bad."

I turn back to the stove where I push the sausage links around the pan with a spatula and hide my smile. "I'll have tea, thanks."

"Toast?" he asks, moving to the toaster after checking the eggs.

"Yes, I'm starved." The thought just pops out.

"I wonder why that is." I don't miss the amusement in Bowen's voice.

Is he flirting with me?

"I like your house. It's very you."

"So, you mean I'm simple and devoid of much personality." He chuckles.

I turn, eyeing him. "No, I mean it's clean, masculine but comfortable, you have a few photos of your family and an award from the firehouse. Plus, there are books on men's hair styling on the bookcase, and a signed jersey from Roberto Clemente hanging like a shrine above your TV. It's neat but contains all the subjects you hold most dear. Which aren't many, that's why they're special. So yes, I like your house."

My answer stuns him into silence, and he sulks around the kitchen until breakfast is done cooking.

After the table is set and Bowen sets down our steaming mugs, coffee for him and tea for me, we sit across from each other.

The clock on the kitchen wall ticks as I try not to stare at him, but there are words buzzing on my tongue, wanting to be set free.

"Just start, Lily. I know you want to ask me things." Those clear blue eyes seem to sigh with resignation.

"Do you really blame yourself for the accident?" I start with a harsh one, but who cares anymore?

If I only get to do this once, might as well get all the ugly stuff out on the table.

"Yes. And no. Logically, I know I didn't cause it. But I'll never forgive myself for your seatbelt not being on."

My cheeks burst into flames at his admission. "That was my fault, not yours, Bowen. I was misbehaving, trying to be bold. And I caught shit for it."

He gives me a wry smile. "You've got curse words this morning, huh?"

"When I'm emotional, I can't help it. But I mean it, none of it was your fault."

There is a pause while we eat the breakfast we cooked together, and as I let his answer sink into my brain.

"Were you ... okay, after? No lingering side effects?" This man looks small, cautious.

I give him a reassuring smile. "Absolutely none. I'm healthy as an ox. Well, except when it rains. Then the places where I had stitches always ache."

A sharp intake of breath. "Me too."

Bowen rubs his neck, and my hand flies reflexively to my right wrist, thumbing the spot where I had twenty stitches. They're our shared battle wounds.

"Do you remember it? The accident?" Bowen asks me a question again before I can ask him one.

I shake my head. "Not fully, no. Bits and pieces, but one second I was in the car, and next I was waking up in a hospital bed. Do you remember it?"

His fingers flex on the table, and I see the tension creep into his jaw. "Probably best that you don't remember. And yes, I do."

"Do you hate me for ending your baseball career?" I choke out.

It's always been a sticking point for me, one I've never been able to get over. He was destined for greatness, and the night of the accident changed all that.

"Never. I've never hated you, not for one second. It still hurts that I lost those opportunities. But I guess I'll never know. Maybe it wasn't meant to happen, one way or another. I'm not unhappy, though, Lily."

The small smile he sends across the table makes my heart rest a little easier. We take a break for a minute, sipping from our mugs and chewing as we watch each other.

I take a deep breath, knowing that the worst question was about to come out of my mouth.

"Why did you leave Fawn Hill? Why weren't you there when I woke up?" This is the big one.

No matter what his answer is, I know it's going to feel like taking a bullet.

Bowen sighs, setting his fork down. "Lily, I can't tell you that. I just ... can't. It's not something you want to hear, and I'm not ... I can't share it."

My head hangs low, devastation creeping up my neck. Last night changed nothing. I thought, for a moment there, that we were really being honest. That everything that's transpired between us was going to be explained. This is the most crucial question, the one that's haunted me for years.

"Would you take this kind of answer?" Bowen reaches across the table, grasping my hand. "I ... I've tried for a very long time to stay away from you. For reasons I can't share. But last night ... it changed a lot. And despite what might happen, I don't want to keep staying away. You were right, Lily. I never stopped having feelings for you. But we're ... complicated. And there is a lot of hurt between us. I never wanted that. And now I want ... hell, so many things. I'm all fucked up."

"Listen to you, waxing poetic. I don't think I've ever heard you describe your feelings so at length."

He shrugs. "I've picked up a few skills in the years we've been apart. Plus, I'm trying harder not to be an asshole."

"You were never an asshole."

Something clouds his eyes. "I never meant to hurt you."

I nod my head, my heart expanding to four times its size. And I'm confused too. I don't want to walk away from this because I'm still in love with him. But I'm also terrified of what he can't tell me. Or how he might desert me once more.

"I know. So, let's ... see where this goes. To taking it slow?"

Raising my mug, I will him to meet me halfway in a toast.

After a minute Bowen raises his. "To taking it slow."

21

BOWEN

And just like that, it's my brother's wedding weekend.

The entire summer seems like a whirlwind, what with my best man duties, usual workload, and chaos with Lily. Add in the news that Lewis Mider landed me a job interview with a Triple-A team in Virginia, and the days seemed to be getting shorter and shorter.

Ever since the night at my place and our talk the subsequent morning, things have been different between Lily and I. Understandably, since we laid it all out there.

Well, not all of it. I was still guarding the secret that would eventually lead to her hating me.

But for now, our interactions were ... civil. More than, actually. We'd even shared some texts, a cup of coffee, and some heavy petting at her place in these last two weeks leading up to the wedding. I'd meant it when I said I wanted things to change, but slowly.

Once I'd kissed her, been inside her, I knew there was no way I could avoid her anymore. I'd had her, and one taste after I'd starved myself for ten years would never be enough. Honestly, nothing would ever be enough. Until I had a ring on her finger and she was tied to me, and even then it wouldn't be enough.

But I knew I'd never get that. So I'd lie to myself, deny that I was about to shatter my heart again and keep seeing her. Maybe a job in baseball would come through, and I could leave and make it easier on both of us. Not that it would ever be easy, but the distance might help.

I'd been in love with Lily for thirteen years, and in the ten we hadn't been together, that love never waned. It might seem impossible, but it hadn't. And it wouldn't go away if I left, but I could shield her from the hurt that was coming if she ever knew the secret I couldn't share.

"Do you think I should bang Presley's friend, Ryan?"

Forrest looks across the room, contemplating the leggy woman with bobbed black hair. She's standing with Presley and Hattie, Presley's grandmother, sipping on a glass of wine.

"You want to fuck a guy?" Fletcher asks, not bothering to look up from his phone.

I check to see what he's doing, but he's only playing Candy Crush. Ever since Keaton gave our family some reading materials on how to support a family member fresh out of rehab, I've been trying to keep an eye on Fletch. One of the side effects of quitting one addiction is picking up another, and gambling can be a go-to for those trying to stay sober from drugs and alcohol.

"No, dipshit, Ryan is a girl. Well, damn, a woman. Would you check out the legs on her?" Fletcher whistles low.

He makes more noise than intended though because said woman directs her gaze to us and raises an eyebrow at my little brother.

Fletcher finally looks up from his game and across the room to Ryan, who is looking at us. His eyes cloud and he taps his fingers on his legs. Interesting.

"I mean, we're both coders. She's gotta be whip-smart. And

she looks like she could either hand me my balls or take real good care of them."

"You're a pig." I snort, hitting him upside the back of the head. "Plus, you're not a coder. You're a hacker."

Forrest rubs his scalp. "Ouch, you prick. And don't talk to grown-ups about subjects you know nothing about."

Fletcher snickers. "He's gonna beat your ass for that one. When are we released from this prison, by the way? I want to go home."

The diner is basically empty a half hour after Keaton and Presley's rehearsal dinner. I'll admit it was a fun night, one I hadn't particularly been keen on since, you know, a room full of strangers isn't exactly my scene. Presley's family, and ours have been coming into town by the carful, even though Keaton claimed they were keeping it small. There were probably forty people at the rehearsal dinner, and there will be double that number tomorrow.

My brother and his bride look so damn happy, it's hard not to feel the love. Which is why I haven't been able to stop staring at Lily all night. Although, I'm never able to stop looking at her once we're within fifty feet of each other.

We've been sneaking glances all night and continue to do so as I watch her walk up to the other women and Ryan.

"Your brother is getting married, stop being selfish," Forrest chides him, interrupting my thoughts about Lily.

"You're the one talking about fucking half the bridesmaids." Fletcher snorts.

Forrest raises his beer, takes a sip. "Not half, just one. We don't get many city girls in Fawn Hill, and Keaton stole the last one. I think I might need to see what big brother is always bragging about."

That makes me laugh. "Keaton never kisses and tells, so stop that noise. Also, you would sleep with anyone at this wedding if they threw a glance your way. You're telling me that you wouldn't drop trou for Penelope if she crooked her finger at you?"

Forrest clams up, taking another sip as his body goes rigid. What the hell is this about? I have a sneaking suspicion I know what's up, because my little brother never shuts his damn mouth. Unless he's done something really bad.

"Don't tell me you—"

"Hey guys, thanks for waiting around." Keaton approaches us, his golden boy looks finely pressed this evening.

He's in an immaculate navy suit, hair slicked back, and he's holding three gift bags stuffed with tissue paper.

"I got you each a gift, to say thank you for not only being my groomsman but for being my brothers." He hands them out.

"Look at you getting all sentimental and shit," Fletcher cracks, making a kissy face at Keaton.

I take my bag from my older brother, and when the twins start rooting around inside, I do the same. I'm not expecting what I pull out.

"You got us ... bracelets?" Forrest eyes him curiously?

It's essentially a thick, gunmetal-colored metal band with a clasp made of black leather. There are tiny dots etched into it, but other than that, it's pretty plain.

"This is ... cool, man," I say, trying to mask my confusion about why he got us matching bracelets.

Keaton pulls up his sleeve, and I see he's wearing an identical one. "Look closer."

I inspect the bracelet again, and this time, something clicks for me. "Wait, these aren't just dots. This is Morse code."

Fletcher starts to laugh. "Oh my God, like the time we only communicated in Morse code for like two months and drove mom crazy!"

We all crack up because that shit was funny. We all love and fear our mother, but we were shithead little boys who liked to cause trouble. Keaton taught us all Morse code as a prank when I was about fourteen and the twins were ten, so we'd have our own secret language.

"Okay, so that's an ... N." Forrest looks around the band, trying to decode it.

"It says Nash Brothers." Fletcher blinks up at Keaton.

It takes him less than a minute to translate it, faster than I could have done, and I find that now that his mind is clear, my little brother is more intelligent than any of us. The wedding gift he built for Presley and Keaton, hell, it's magnificent.

I clear my throat, surprised by the emotion in it. "This is really nice, Keat. Thank you."

"Dad would have loved these." Forrest is oddly humbled for once in his life.

We all sit in silence for a minute, and I think every one of us is fully aware that we wish Dad could be here. Even with what he did to "protect" me from Senator Grantham, I miss my father every single day.

"All right, no more sappiness." Keaton sucks a breath in, smiling. "I want you all to get a good night of sleep, we have a wedding to pull off tomorrow."

We all nod, standing to hug our oldest brother for the gift and then disperse.

And I head right for the girl I've been sneaking smiles with all night.

22

LILY

The rehearsal dinner is at Kip's per Presley's request because Hattie is hosting it and we already all know the food is dynamite.

Penelope and I spend the day turning the old diner into a lovebird's paradise; white lace tablecloths, pink and white flowers covering any surface we could stick them, Etsy-worthy signage, and a big wooden ... well, creation is the only word for it, that Fletcher made.

I have to say; I did not know Fletcher could make anything ... besides a mess. That was mean but true. In the last year I'd seen him really trying, and when he'd shown up with this beautiful gift he wanted to present at the rehearsal dinner, I actually cried.

Penelope did, too. What the heck had gotten into that girl?

The work of art was a seven-foot-tall wooden ladder that he'd carved and made look completely rustic. It could be used for throw blanket storage, or to hang coffee mugs from the branches he'd whittled onto it, or just as a piece of decor. The part that made me burst into tears, though? Hanging from each rung were these hand-carved wooden signs of places that were near and dear to Presley and Keaton, along with their mileage from Fawn Hill. New York City, the town in Connecticut where Presley had grown up, the town Keaton went to college, the island they planned to honeymoon on. And on the middle rung was Fawn Hill ... but instead of the mileage, it simply said, *home*.

Gosh, I could sob just thinking about it. It was beautiful, a one-of-a-kind gift made with love.

Dinner had gone well, with Presley's father giving a nice speech as they're the ones who had footed the bill. Traditionally, the groom's family was supposed to have this honor, but since Presley didn't have the closest relationship with her parents, she and Keaton had flipped the script. They wanted Eliza and Hattie to give toasts at the wedding reception, and those two were the ones who'd been around for much of the planning. Presley's parents didn't seem to mind, and so far, her mother and sister had behaved themselves, so I didn't have to give anyone the maid of honor beatdown.

Wine and beer had flown freely, out-of-town guests had been introduced or reconnected, and all in all, it had been a night of merriment. If not a blur for me. Being a maid of honor was no joke, and I was getting a crash course in hospitality with the job. My goal was to keep Presley free of worry and drama, and out of any technical details so she could enjoy the entire weekend. Not that she was a bridezilla by any means, but she and Keaton deserved to soak up as much couple time in the next two days as they were able to.

And now, Kip's is almost empty, save for immediate family and bridal party members. I'm standing with Presley, Hattie, and the third bridesmaid, Ryan, who is Presley's best friend from New York City.

Ryan is ... my opposite. In a good way, I genuinely like her. But the girl is crazy with a capital *C*. She handles whiskey like a Southern gentleman, has no filter, wore a black silk slip dress, that looks like it's better suited to the bedroom, to the rehearsal dinner, and has no problem striking up a conversation with anyone.

"So, which Nash brother is on the table for me to sleep with tomorrow?" She hooks her long, thin arm around Presley's shoulder.

Oh, did I mention she looks like a Victoria's Secret model? One of the ones from the nineties, all natural puffy lips and perfectly rounded thighs.

"The twins are single, but they're children." Presley snorts.

"How about lumberjack brooder over there? He looks yummy." She licks her lips as her gaze travels to Bowen.

My veins singe with jealousy, and I'm speaking before I even know what I'm doing. "He's off limits."

Presley looks smugly satisfied that I claimed Bowen, and Ryan holds up her hands in surrender. "It's cool, Lily Pad, you can have the hot fireman. I like to toy with boys … maybe I'll give Coder McGee over there a whirl."

Ryan and Forrest might make a good match, but it would probably end in disaster. "Forrest is all yours."

"It's a good weekend to be a Nash man." Hattie chuckles. "If you aren't getting married, you're part of the meat market swap. It's a win all around."

"Grandma!" Presley laughs, hugging her grandmother.

"Who knew there was a coven of hot men in this small town? It's like *Twilight*, but they aren't sucking the life out of your neck. Or maybe they are. Could be hot." Ryan shrugs.

I feel a hand on my elbow and look up, Presley's face turning to the visitor, too.

"Oh, hi." I breathe, seeing Bowen standing beside me.

It's hard to suck oxygen into my body when he's so close, wearing a suit no less. Gosh, he's so ruggedly handsome it should be illegal. Women everywhere are in danger of passing out when this man cleans up for a fancy dinner.

"Thank you for tonight, Bowie." Presley winks at him, using the nickname his brothers call him that he hates.

"You're joining the family tomorrow, so I guess I'll put up with that bullshit right now. But once you're a full-fledged Nash, don't think I won't pull pranks if you keep the Bowie crap up," Bowen jokes with her.

Presley looks between us, her smile turning to a scheming smirk. "Noted. Now, why doesn't the best man walk my maid of honor home? Make sure she gets there safe?"

I roll my eyes at her, knowing exactly what she's getting at. I haven't told her, or anyone really, what's been happening with Bowen. I didn't want to spoil one of the most important times in her life, especially if things turned sour between her soon-to-be brother-in-law and me before the wedding day. No one needed our drama in their lives. Heck, I didn't even need our drama, but I loved the man so what was I supposed to do?

"I would be honored to." Bowen holds out his arm.

Presley looks like she might keel over, so shocked that her plan worked that I kind of want to get her a wet washcloth for her head. I smirk, turning to walk away with Bowen. When I look back over my shoulder, her jaw is still unhinged, her mouth ready to catch flies.

The minute I looped my arm through his arm, I got shocked, jumping a bit. "I must have static, sorry."

Bowen steers me away from the group, bending down to whisper in my ear. "Or we just have a spark."

I flush with desire. One sentence from him and I turn to a puddle of lust. How has he always had this effect on me?

"This best man gig has given you some confidence," I joke as we walk to the door to exit Kip's.

Main Street is quiet, with most of Fawn Hill having locked their doors and gone to sleep now that it's well past ten p.m. Bowen and I walk next to each other, not touching but our steps and our bodies in rhythm. It feels intimate, walking alone down the streets we grew up on. They know so much of our history, are part of the landscape of our relationship.

"I've always had confidence; you just haven't seen it in a while." He smirks.

"No, I haven't. It's ... attractive," I confess, butterflies fluttering in my stomach.

"You look beautiful." Bowen's gaze warms my face.

His compliment sends tingles through my body. "It's just the dress ... I wouldn't normally wear something so tight ..."

I skim my hands down the burnt orange fit and flare dress that falls to my mid-calf. It's a corset design on top, and I'm showing more cleavage than I have in years, but I fell in love with the unique design and had to wear it.

"Notice how I didn't say tonight? You don't look beautiful *tonight*. You look beautiful all the time. I can never seem to keep my eyes off you."

I blink at him as we turn off Main Street and into the neighborhood that funnels out into streets beyond, one of those being my condo community. Bowen is charming tonight, and something about the wedding gives a rose-colored tint to the world. Nothing bad can happen this weekend, and the love that's always existed between us is a stronger force than I've felt in a long time.

"You're making me blush." I smile, looking away.

"Good. You deserve to be told. I ... regret not being able to tell you every day of the past ten years." He reaches for my hand.

I lace my fingers through his, loving the feel of his rough calluses beneath.

"Can I say something without sounding ... insensitive?" I proceed cautiously.

"Of course." His head dips, the long dark mop on the top of his head falling out of its carefully created swoop.

"This is weird." I giggle nervously.

Bowen chuckles too. "I know."

"I'm used to you avoiding me. To thinking that you hate me. We fell into this pattern of smoldering avoidance, with tense interactions and now ..."

"Now we're holding hands while I walk you home?"

"Yes!" I say, laughing more. "It's just *weird*."

"But good weird?" Bowen asks.

"Yes, good weird. But it feels like I'm in some kind of time warp. As if no years have passed us by at all. Is it possible to feel this connected after what's happened between us?"

He glances out into the darkness as we turn onto the court where my townhouse is, a pensive look on his face. I take the couple of seconds he's quiet with his thoughts to admire the steel cut of his jaw. And the way his eyelashes are long and almost girlish, the only feminine attribute he possesses.

"I think, that if you share something as strong as we do, it's possible."

Bowen doesn't say the word love, but he might as well have. My heart pounds in my chest, and before I realize where we are, the three steps up to my front door appear at my feet.

His hand unlatches from mine, but instead of dropping to his side, it travels up my wrist and to my shoulder, where he uses it to pull me in closer.

"I'm not going to ask to come up or accept an invite to. I said I'd walk you home, and we're taking it slow. Doesn't mean I don't want to, though."

Bowen's blue eyes flash in the dark as he says this last part. It makes all the parts south of my waist tingle with anticipation. Of *next time*.

"I'll see you tomorrow?" I swallow after asking the dumb question because my throat is dry and of course I'll see him tomorrow.

He bends, sweeping his lips over mine in a half-kiss. There is no pressure in it, and the kiss to my forehead he follows it up with almost feels more intimate than me naked in his bed.

"Good night, beautiful."

I'm left standing dumbfounded on my stoop.

The angry, monosyllabic Bowen Nash has disappeared. And in his wake, he's left the sweet, charming high school sweetheart version that I fell in love with.

I'm not sure who is more dangerous to my heart.

23

BOWEN

My night of sleep was fitful, and I tossed and turned with the taste of Lily's skin on my lips.

It wasn't the bad kind of restless, but the excited kind. The first-day-of-school kind, the Christmas-morning kind, the championship-game kind.

Because I was anticipating the moment I was in right now. Which was watching Lily walk down the aisle.

As a man, I've never really dreamed about my wedding day. Back in high school, I knew I wanted to be with Lily for the rest of my life. I'd been a young, cocky prick with a hot arm, but I knew she was my forever girl. That being said ... I had no picture in my head of what us getting married would look like. It was a far-off idea, someday that I'd let her plan and show up for.

But seeing her come toward me in the pink, wispy dress that floated around her body ... she looked like an angel. My heart was spasming, going haywire in my chest.

Keaton looks back at me from his premier spot on the altar and winks. I nod and try to hide my smile, because really ... no one has any idea what's going on with us. Oh, I'm sure my older brother has his suspicions, but this is his day and I'm not going to burden him with my confusing life.

Lily blushes as my eyes scan down the length of her body, pausing on the way her hips shift, on her perky, round breasts, and then up, to meet those dark, shining blue orbs. Her hair is twisted up into some braided, fairy-like do, and the whole ensemble makes her look like one of those fairies described in a children's storybook.

Once she's standing on the other side of the altar, it's difficult to keep my eyes off her. But I know my gaze needs to be directed straight, to Presley walking down the aisle to her groom. I need to focus on being the best man. Getting Lily out of that dress will be the first priority once my duties for the day are over.

It's inevitable we'll end up back in one of our hotel rooms tonight. And Lily may think nothing of spending time together tonight, but I have to be careful. There are many Fawn Hill residents at this wedding, and we all know the gossip runs rampant. It only takes one word along that game of telephone for it to get back to Senator Grantham.

And I don't need that prick coming into my shop again, threatening me about the pact he and my father made.

The wedding guests sitting in the pews stand as Presley prepares to walk down the aisle. Hattie is escorting her, which I thought might be a sign of disrespect to her father, but apparently, he doesn't mind.

Both of the women are beaming, Presley in her white gown and Hattie in her beige women's suit. My gaze swings to my brother, who is...

Keaton is crying. Actual tears are shining in his eyes, and he's biting his lip as if he's trying not to break down like a baby. A lump of emotion forms in my throat, and dammit, these people are basically making my balls shrivel up.

When Presley reaches Keaton, he kisses Hattie on the cheek,

and she hands him his bride. It's all very formal, but each action has significance. They stand together as the priest goes through the service, the vows, and then finally they're kissing.

"Friends and family, may I present, Mr. and Mrs. Keaton Nash!"

The priest introduces them for the first time, and then my brother and his wife are sauntering down the aisle arm in arm, with smiles so wide their cheeks must ache.

It's my turn to step down from the altar and take my designated bridesmaid back to the vestibule of the church. Lily meets me in the middle, her eyes shiny with tears.

The minute I touch her, standing here in the spot where we likely would have gotten married, it's like the whole world disappears. We pause, staring at each other. The life we should have had flashes in front of me. Marriage, children, different careers.

"Hey, buddy, stop mooning and walk up the damn aisle, you're holding us up." Forrest jabs me in the ribs with his elbow, and I'm knocked sharply into reality.

I smile at Lily, covering up the heaviness that weighs on my mind and extend my arm to her. She takes it, and they fit perfectly together.

I don't miss the way some guests watch us as we walk toward Keaton and Presley, who are getting ready for their receiving line.

As soon as we take our places in line, I turn to Forrest and whisper, "I need a drink."

He looks to his left, at Penelope, and turns back to face me. "You and me both, brother."

The night has turned into a blur.

With our joint-brother toast done and over, dinner eaten, and the first dances out of the way, we're all free and clear to get wasted.

And that's exactly what I've done. Family members from out-of-town keep getting rounds of shots, my wine glass was never empty during dinner, and cocktail hour saw me nursing two glasses of whiskey.

The liquor, and watching Lily in a church during a wedding, even if it wasn't ours, is messing with me. I'm being sloppy, even though I promised myself I wouldn't publicly grope or flirt with the maid of honor in this wedding.

But she's gorgeous, and dancing, and smiling as she laughs and it's impossible to stay away from her.

Which is why we've basically been glued together on the dance floor for the last hour. My hands on her hips, her fingers tangling in my hair. Lily's been pulling me by the tie, jokingly being seductive, and more than once, my cock has been ground into her ass.

I'm too buzzed to notice the strange, almost jaw-dropping looks we're collecting, but I know people are in fact looking. But this is happening, and I'm a fool for thinking that we could just take things slow. Hiding our relationship was never going to work, not when people have watched us like hawks for ten years when we *weren't* involved.

"What is happening?" Fletcher muses as he watches Lily hook me like a fish on the dance floor.

"We've been transported from Keaton's wedding to some alternate universe." Penelope throws her body around, dancing like a maniac as she cackles.

I'm not much of a dancer. Hell, I'd say that nobody in this room aside from Lily has ever seen me dance. I don't like to do it.

But give me a whole bottle of liquor, practically, and I'll make a fool of myself.

Shimmying across the center of the floor, as if I'm a fish on the line, I jump on over to Lily. By the time I scoop her up in my arms, my brothers and the bridesmaids are hysterically laughing at me.

And it's so much fun, I don't even care.

Lily giggles into my neck, and I carry her off the floor, needing a drink. Of water? I probably should. But most likely, it'll be whiskey.

Setting her down, I have to steady her as she stumbles on flat feet. She took those sexy heels off an hour ago, much to my dismay.

"You're drunk." I chuckle, seeing through booze goggles myself.

"And you're handsome." Lily winks at me.

I forgot how flirty she is when she gets a little alcohol in her. Typically, Lily is reserved and friendly. She's not very sarcastic and is kind to her core. But when you give her some drinks ... that saucy side comes out.

We're kind of similar in that way because the introvert I've morphed into seems to become a fun alter-ego when there is whiskey involved.

I palm her waist, the darkness of the corner shadowing us, and back her up into the wall. "Good thing I found the maid of honor before midnight."

"Why? Am I going to turn into a pumpkin or something?" She snickers.

I smooth my hand down her cheek. "No ... I ..."

Lily cracks up as I can't seem to remember my train of thought.

"Well, I was going to say that the best man has to take the maid of honor home, but I forget where I was bringing midnight into play? Either way, I think we're supposed to have wedding sex. It's one of our duties."

She nods solemnly. "Is that so?"

"It is decidedly so." I bend, my lips so close to hers.

"Now you sound like a Magic 8 ball." Her giggles hit my mouth.

"And you smell delicious," I whisper right before I cover that mouth with mine.

Our train of thought makes no sense, but the tingling longing that's been stemming from my cock all night flares with desire when Lily's tongue invades my mouth.

We're making out like teenagers in the shadows of a crowded room, and it feels so illicit and *hungry* that when my brain begs for me to press my hips into her core, I do.

Lily groans into my mouth, one leg raising to hook around my hip. I catch it, her dress sliding up until my fingers stroke silky skin.

The change of a song catches my ear, and I break our foreplay off with a rasping breath.

"We need to get out of here before I fuck you in public right on top of the head table."

Those sapphire eyes turn molten, and I grab her hand before either of us can rethink this.

24

BOWEN

The hotel room door slams into the wall as we bust through it.

"Thank goodness Keaton was such an ass about making everyone stay in the hotel." Lily giggles as she kicks her heels off.

I'm wrenching my tie from my neck, fumbling to uncoil it and throw it across the room. "Fuck, he was a prick about that. I'll have to thank him."

We're doing a drunk tango through the short entryway in my queen-size deluxe, the only room that was left by the time Keaton put his foot on my metaphorical neck and forced me to get a room within the block. The Queen Anne Inn was the only hotel for twenty miles around Fawn Hill and was located exactly five minutes from the wedding venue, which was also five minutes from my house. It was ridiculous to have us pay to stay here, but Presley had expressed to my brother how fun it would be if everyone woke up in the same place the morning after the wedding and ate brunch together. And what Presley thought would be fun, was Keaton's job to make happen.

Now, though, I was going to have to pat my brother on the back.

"Why do you have so many buttons?" Lily whines as she hastily works her way down the white shirt under my tux.

"And how the heck do these straps work?" I growl, frustrated that her skin is encased in so much fabric.

The buzz of the many drinks consumed at the wedding flows through my veins, charging the sexual energy between us just a little bit more than normal. Being under the influence of alcohol makes being under the influence of Lily that much more intoxicating. I don't need to think. Not about the ramifications of pinning her beneath me, or about what we'll tell everyone who saw us almost making out on the dance floor, or about the threats her father's made against me.

My inhibitions are nonexistent, and that means I can focus solely on giving Lily pleasure and taking it in return.

"*Yes*," Lily moans the second she's freed my abs from the shirt.

I shuck my jacket off, the shirt follows, and then I'm standing there while her fingers explore my pecs and torso. Her hands are small and soft, lighting a path of fire everywhere they touch.

Grabbing her behind the neck, I crush her to my chest, unable to fight off the urge my lips have to be on hers any longer. Cherries, a bite of whiskey and the tail end of a spicy vermouth. Lily was drinking Manahttans toward the end of the night, and now they're on my tongue.

I want to drown in her taste.

"Need to taste you," I husk out.

Her voice is barely audible. "You already are."

Lifting her from the waist, I deposit her on the bed in a cloud of pink wisp as her dress flies around her.

"I've tasted your mouth. Now, I need to taste your sweet pussy."

My cock hardens impossibly more at my own words, and Lily whimpers as her head hits the mattress with a light thud. I can't resist unzipping myself, the haze of booze spurring me on, and pushing my dress pants down over my hips. My rigid cock springs free, and I hiss as it makes contact with the air. All the blood in my body seems to zero in on this one appendage, and my hand instinctively reaches down to stroke.

Lily is mesmerized as I jack myself in front of her, my balls tightening with every pull.

"If you aren't out of that dress in three seconds, I'm going under that skirt and can't be held responsible if it ends up in shreds on the floor." My voice is clipped and brute.

She scrambles up, shrugging out of the gown and kicking it off the bed. And then there she is, naked save for a scrap of white lace hiding the lips I want to taste so badly.

Lunging for the bed, I kick away the last of my clothing and rip off her thong, wrapping my meaty arms around her slim waist.

As the lace tears, Lily gasps. "I thought that only happened in books or movies. It didn't even hurt."

Striking while her eyes are round and innocent, I lower my head. "No, but this might."

My teeth clamp around her clit, sucking it in, and she rears up off the bed. "BOWEN!"

I don't let up. My lips suck at her sensitive nub, stopping only to fuck her deep with my tongue. I feel her shake just seconds after I first tasted her, and by the way her hands are fisting in the sheets, I can tell she is about to come. I've studied Lily for years. I was the first boy to kiss her, to feel her body, to take her in a way so intimate and trusting that I'm honored she gave me that gift.

The signs of her orgasm are something I memorized a long

time ago, and I plan to see them over and over before this night is through.

"Come for me, baby." I milk her, giving her everything I've got.

Her head thrashes on the bed, and she's mewling so loudly that I hope the people in the room next to us can hear her.

She's teetering on the edge, and the moment I press two fingers inside her as I lave my tongue over her clit, she falls. Scratching at my arms and hair, muttering my name, flexing her hips over and over ... Lily is a sight to behold. The alcohol has freed her too, from shame and self-consciousness.

I prowl up the bed toward her, not bothering to stop to see if she needs a minute. No, I know she can handle this. I drive right into her, my dick slicking all the way in, right up until my balls nestle between her ass.

"*Fuck*, baby." My forehead drops to her shoulder as all of Lily's limbs latch onto me.

Her legs pretzel around my waist, her arms secure around my neck. She's holding on in preparation for the storm about to savage her. Because once I pull out again, I'm not stopping until we're both crying with release.

My retreat is slow, and I savor every sensation as my cock slides from within her. With my throbbing head poised at her entrance once more, I lift my chin to look her in the eyes.

"You're the most beautiful fucking thing I've ever seen in my life. I could die right now and have so many regrets about us, but at least I'd be with you."

Those blue eyes shine in the muted light of the hotel room, and before Lily can say anything else, I slam into her.

This moment is endless. It could be hours or years as I pound into her, begging for both of our climaxes, but I can't even tell which way is up. All I see is her, the girl I've loved for my entire life. The one I'd love for a hundred lifetimes if I was lucky enough.

The realization dawns as my come shoots deep inside her, and I can barely remember my own name, let alone the reasons we shouldn't be together.

I love Lily. Why should I have to hide a love that goes so far beyond the word, there isn't even a definition for it?

25

LILY

The two weeks after Presley and Keaton's wedding goes by in a blur.

When I'm not at the library working my full-time job, I'm filling in for Presley and teaching classes or helping with admin work at the yoga studio.

With September hitting and the town's children going back to school, my day job is stressful and packed. We have all kinds of beginning of the year projects planned with the school district, plus I typically meet with all the underprivileged families who are gifted their textbooks and reading material for free from the library. The initiative is one I put together almost two years ago and wanted to.

I'm working around the clock, and you'd think that would be enough, but somehow, my father has roped me back into political appearances. I know I'd told him off at the dinner in Philadelphia, said I'd never go to another one of those again, but ...

I'm weak. I love my parents, and I've been a part of their machine far longer than I've had my own life and my own home. Their game is the one I know, and sometimes, I can't help but fall back into it. Go to an event, be doted on by my father. Show up at an appearance, see that smile of gratitude and respect on my mom's face.

And on top of it all, I'm trying to keep up some semblance of a ... can I call it a relationship? Well, whatever is happening, Bowen and I have tried to carve out an hour here and there for each other. After the night of drunken wedding sex, which was, *gosh* ...

I blush just thinking about how wild it was.

"What are you smirking at?" Presley asks as I cut up cheese to put on our charcuterie board.

She's finally back from her and Keaton's Hawaiian honeymoon, and Penelope begged for a girl's night the minute I'd had a day to fully sleep and recover from the marathon I'd been sprinting.

We sit around Presley's dining room table, chatting about the wedding, her honeymoon, what's been going on in Fawn Hill and everything in between.

"Yeah, what's so funny?" Penelope accuses.

"Nothing." I try to clamp my lips shut, but the smile just won't stop.

Presley tickles my side. "Out with it!"

Here goes nothing. At least Keaton is out on a vet emergency call right now, and not here to witness this.

"Bowen and I ... we slept together." I wring my hands, waiting for the outburst.

"I KNEW IT!" Penelope shouts, jumping up and running around the table in circles.

Presley just smiles and sips her white wine. "It was only a matter of time."

I know I look guilty now. "Well, we've actually been seeing each other. And the wedding wasn't the ... uh, first time."

"What?" Now Presley is acting like a squawking chicken. "You've been having sex with Bowen for how long?"

The two of them are looking at each other like the world has just exploded, or pigs are flying, or ... Brad Pitt just showed up in Keaton and Presley's living room. Now that would be a hoot.

"Sit down." I laugh, both shy about having this conversation but relieved to get this off my chest.

"I'm sweating." Penelope huffs out a breath. "This is giving me so much life."

"All right, are you two going to listen?" I chuckle.

"Yes, spill." Presley perks up like a good little pupil, all ears.

"Well, it started the night of the meth house fire."

"When I texted you?" Presley interrupts.

"Yes, I ... well, I went over to his house to wait for him. I don't know why, it was such a stupid move, but we ended up spending the night together."

Presley leans toward Penelope. "Secretly, I schemed that plan in my head. I knew it was a long shot, but now that it actually worked, I think I should go into the matchmaking business or something."

My jaw dislodges. "You sneaky little ... you were trying to get us together?"

"Obviously, I was!" She pumps her fist as if she's scored a touchdown or a goal.

"If your dating magic is that spot on, maybe you can wish Jake Gyllenhaal into my life?" Penelope pops an olive in her mouth.

"Shut it, let her talk." Presley slathers spicy jam onto a breadstick while silencing our other best friend, then motions for me to continue.

"Actually, if I'm being honest, it started in the early part of the summer, even before you got engaged. Bowen picked me up on the side of the road after my car broke down, and things just kind of spiraled from there. We kept bumping into each other, and I'm sure part of your diabolical plan included making us best man and maid of honor because it worked."

Presley looks down, a smirk gracing her lips, all but confirming her meddling. Penelope slaps her on the back in congratulations.

"And then we just ... decided to take things slow. We've had some talks about the past, about the accident, although there are still things he isn't willing to tell me. We've obviously been sleeping together."

"How is the sex?" Penelope interrupts as if this is the most important part of the conversation.

I tip my chin and give her an admonishing look.

She shrugs her shoulders innocently. "What? Is this girl talk or not? You haven't fucked the man since you were seventeen, and he is a *man*. A firefighting man. It's gotta be fantastic? Is it fantastic?"

I have to laugh at her, she's incorrigible. But I nod. "I can confirm that it's fantastic."

She fans her face. "Oh, girl, tell me more."

"No, tell us about the *relationship*." Presley glares at the horn-dog at the table.

"Well ... I don't even know that I can call it that? We haven't had that talk yet although I know where I want it to go. I don't know, it's just been so long and I know there is still so much to talk about between us and I can't ... my head is just a mess."

"Do you still love him?" Presley asks.

"Of course, I do. That's never been the problem. The issue is that for ten years, he's ignored me. He left me while I was still in the hospital and has never told me why. Even now, he doesn't want to talk about it, and he barely wants me telling people. And before you ask, no, Bowen hasn't explicitly said not to tell anyone. But we only spend time with each other in the privacy of our own homes. In the months we've been taking it slow, he hasn't asked me out to dinner once, or dropped by the library unannounced, or gone to the movies together ... or anything. I feel like a booty call or a secret mistress."

"And that's why you're telling us now. Because you know that it can't continue like this." Penelope nods, knowing me better than I know myself. "You've waited too long to get him back, so you want it to last. But, Lil ... not like this. If he is going to pull some fuckboy bullshit with you, you have to end it."

She's harsh, but she's right.

"All right, hold on. Before we go Carrie Underwood on his tires, can we make some sane suggestions?" Presley smirks at Penelope and then turns to me. "Talk to him about it. Tell him how you're feeling."

"I already have. I've tried ..."

"But if you're not happy with how he's responding, then don't put up with it. You've waited this long for Bowen to come around, and if it's not in the right way, you still have nothing to lose. That might be mean, but you deserve answers. And if he isn't willing to give them, then you can survive it. You've gone through it once and come out stronger. You're a different woman than the girl who lost him back then. Show him that."

They're both right. Even if we've been getting to know each other again, even if every moment of passion and fleeting happiness is worth it right now, eventually the doubts will crowd my thoughts. I won't be able to move past our history if Bowen doesn't give me the real reason he wasn't there after the accident. And a relationship can't be built on lies. It shouldn't be, and that's what we're doing right now. Putting a Band-Aid over the bullet hole, a temporary hold on a wound that is only growing bigger each time we ignore it.

"Why do these girls' nights always turn into gossiping about boys?" I joke, wanting to change the subject.

They've given me more to think about than I can process right now, and I want to chew it over when I'm alone.

"Because what else do we have to talk about? The fact that Mrs. Murtins, the high school gym teacher, is definitely banging the new math teacher who just moved here from Lancaster?"

"Penelope, I swear, you're the locomotive of the Fawn Hill Rumor Train." Presley giggles. "But, is it really true?"

"Without a doubt, it is. Or so I heard."

"The new math teacher is really nice. He came in to check out some books on World War II for personal reading," I inform them, taking a long sip of my wine now that my relationship discussion is off the table.

"Hot, too. See? Another potential suitor for you to match me up with." Penelope hits Presley in the arm.

"I'll get right on that." She rolls her eyes.

"So, how was the honeymoon?" I ask. "Any babies made?"

Presley coughs on a salted cashew. "Absolutely not. I am so not ready for that. Not with a new business, a new husband, and trying to find a new house."

Her and Keaton's house search has been dismal. Neither can agree on what they want, only that they don't want to stay in Keaton's bachelor pad.

"Yeah, please take your time. You have all the time in the world to have a baby, and then they take it all."

If it were me, I'd be having babies the minute the ring was on my finger. But, that was just me. It had always been my dream to have a big family, to be a mama. I couldn't wait to enjoy all that came along with having children. And not so secretly, I hoped those children were with Bowen.

"What about that house out in the boonies?" Penelope asks.

"We *live* in the boonies, by the way. Most people would consider Fawn Hill *way* out there, coming from the city. But, no, it was too ... I don't know. I just know when I find it, I'll know it's the right house. Kind of like the man. The one. Ya know?"

"I do know." Penelope nods, doing that quiet thing she's done lately. Way more than usual, at least.

"And Ryan got back to New York okay? It was really nice to finally meet her."

And I'm being honest when I say that. She's even more of a spitfire than Penelope, and that's saying something. Her flair for fashion, speaking her mind, telling people off and the ability to read almost anyone, even Bowen, is paired with a kind heart and this innate knack for listening.

"Yeah, she was there for a minute but now I think she's in Brussels. Or maybe it's Calgary? I can never keep track of her world travels. But yes, she's amazing. I'm so glad you guys got to meet her."

Penelope snorts. "Yeah, I think Forrest was happy he got to meet her, too."

Do I detect an edge of bitterness in my best friend's voice?

Presley speaks before I can say anything. "That he was. But he's so not Ryan's type. She may be loud, obnoxious and opinionated herself, but she never dates guys that closely matched to her personality. She and Forrest are too similar. They'd kill each other before the first date was over."

"Funny, that's sometimes how I feel about Forrest, too."

The words slip out of my mouth before I have time to gather them back, and Penelope and Presley's eyes widen, stunned.

I shrug. "What? He's always annoyed me. In a loveable, little brother kind of way."

And then they dissolve into hysterics.

Presley coughs as she tries to talk over her laughter. "Lily Grantham, I didn't know you had a mean bone in your body. I kind of like seeing this side of you."

26

LILY

"So, Presley and Keaton had a nice wedding day?"

My mother sits down at her kitchen table where I'm nursing a cup of tea.

"They did. It was beautiful." I smile, remembering how happy they'd looked as they'd swayed during their first dance.

"I bumped into Dierdra at the grocery store last week, and she said it was lovely." There is a hint of something in her voice that I can't place, and I don't like it.

Maybe she's bitter that she and Dad weren't invited, though I have no clue why they'd be aggravated about that. They were never close with the Nash family even when I was dating Bowen back in high school. And after the accident, things were even more icy. It's not like I'd brought Presley around my parents that much, and she had no obligation to invite them just because I was her maid of honor.

But ... I wouldn't put it past my father to be salty that someone in Fawn Hill didn't invite the resident senator to their wedding, even if they were barely acquaintances.

"That's great." I sip my tea, not giving another inch to wedding talk.

My parents' kitchen was overkill as was everything in their house. Growing up, we lived in a very different home, one I loved and cherished as a child. My childhood home was a three-bedroom ranch right off Main Street. It had shag carpeting and a rooster patterned backsplash in the kitchen. Out back, there had been an old, rusty jungle gym left by the previous owners, and the pipes would freeze every winter. Dad fixed everything by hand and even built a vanity for my mother in her bathroom. My bedroom was pink and I had a canopy bed, and the floors were littered with Barbies, Polly Pockets, and books.

This house? It's a model home for entertaining. Neutral everything, granite everything, shiny tile floors, and top-of-the-line appliances. It felt as warm as a hotel, and my mother employed one of the local cleaning ladies to come in once a week to maintain it. It was cavernous for just the two of them and compared to all the other homes in Fawn Hill; it was obnoxious. They'd knocked down the previous home on the lot and built this McMansion. Of course, there were other large homes in Fawn Hill, but they fit the landscape. My parent's home just looked like a politician's Stepford dream.

My mother deserved for cleaners to come in after everything she'd been through ... the cancer treatments had worked but left her body a shell of its former self, even in remission. But I couldn't lie and say I wasn't disappointed in how she'd allowed my father to transform her from a hard-working, small-town woman with a backbone to a politician's wife. It seemed that she cared more about dinner parties and campaign rallies than she did about living her own life. Part of me wishes that my parents were still the humble, ambitious, bright-eyed innocents who lived in that ranch.

"Oh, come off it, Lily, I know you were seen canoodling with Bowen at the wedding. The town has practically been foaming at the mouth for two weeks."

And there it is. I've been waiting for this moment since the morning I snuck out of Bowen's hotel room, checking if the coast was clear like some sort of turncoat spy.

I sigh. "Yes ... it was ... we had a lot of drinks, Mom."

"Oh, I call bullcrap. You've been lighter than air lately, stood up to your father at a charity dinner, have barely returned my calls for weeks, and now you're seen kissing your ex-boyfriend at his brother's wedding? You're in love, my dear. And I couldn't be happier!"

She claps her hands together like some kind of fairy godmother turning my pumpkin into a carriage. The glee on her face makes me kind of giddy if only for the fact that I love to see her jubilant any time now. My mother deserves it.

And now that she's caught me, there isn't much sense in denying it any further.

I hold my hands up, trying to rein in her excitement just a tad. "Okay, okay ... we've been seeing each other, but—"

"Oh, I knew it! I'm a happy mama, that's for sure. When can we have him over for dinner?" I can tell by her expression that she's already scheming.

"Mom, please slow down. It's early, and there is ... you know the history. We're taking things slow."

"Slow? Honey, you're nearly thirty. It's time to bag that boy for good and give me some grandbabies."

I slap my palm to my forehead. "This is why I wasn't going to tell you."

"Tell her what?" Dad enters the kitchen, all business in a navy striped suit.

"Oh, sweetheart, I didn't think you'd be home for lunch. What can I fix you?" Immediately, Mom rises from her seat and goes to the fridge.

"Do we have any of the leftover meatloaf? I'll take a plate of that. Thanks, darling." Dad kisses her cheek as he passes her and heads toward me to take a seat at the kitchen table. "Now, what weren't you telling your mother?"

I'm about to open my mouth when Mom beats me to the punch. "She and Bowen are dating again! Oh, Eric, I could just float I'm so happy!"

Mom is busy fussing around on the other side of the kitchen, but I'm sitting right across from my father. I see the way his face darkens, how his eyebrows furrow together and his jaw sets with a hard click.

"Is that right?" He nods slowly, his cold, blue eyes focusing on me.

There is something in his expression that has the hair on my arms pricking up, and my heart beating into my throat in a nauseous manner. That feeling of dread, of sick fear, right before something terrible is about to happen ... it fills the air of my kitchen, unbeknownst to my mother. Only I'm privy to it, this primal anger rolling off my father.

In a flash, it's gone, replaced by the smarmy, fake nice politician's smile I've become so accustomed to. "Well, honey, that's great. How did you two get back together? When?"

Something in my gut tells me not to reveal too many details. I've never felt this many alarm bells going off in my head, and heck, this is my father. It's just ... I saw something in him seconds before. Something almost ... evil. I've never had that much split-second intuition in my life, but now I know what it feels like.

"Oh, it's not an uncommon story. Mutual friends, same hangout spots. Old feelings linger like they say. It's nothing serious, just seeing each other."

Lies. Lies. So many lies. My stomach churns with keeping the truth from my parents because the people-pleasing little girl inside me knows that she should seek any method of approval.

But adult me? I'm apprehensive. My guard is up.

My father nods as Mom sets his plate down in front of him and moves to sit on the other side, between us.

"And so, you think this is a good idea?" He's trying not to give his feelings away, but I can hear the disapproval in his words.

"Eric! Naturally, it's a good idea. They love each other." Mom rolls her eyes at him.

My father stops his fork midway to his mouth when she says the word love. He sets it down, looks at me.

"You do remember that this is the boy who almost killed you?"

My skin peppers with goose bumps. "He didn't almost kill me. We were in an unavoidable car crash, and he himself lost a lot that day as well."

It's no secret to me, or to Bowen, or to anyone in Fawn Hill, that my father has never liked Bowen Nash. I remember the arguments we used to get into when I was in high school and blindly in love with Bowen. My father thought he was a bad influence, that he was too old for me, that he was just a jock who was using me for the one thing teenage boys are after. My curfew was limited, I fought with my father about going to the Nash's for dinner, and one time, my father even had the gall to sic the cops on Bowen when he brought me home three minutes too late on the night of his junior prom.

And now this again. After I woke up from my coma, my father didn't start his propaganda against Bowen right away. But he may as well have. Over the course of the next year after the accident, Dad would try to poison my mind and my heart against him. Calling him irresponsible, a degenerate, reckless, and dangerous. Any chance he could, my father would remind me that Bowen abandoned me in the hospital, and until Penelope set me straight, he even tried to convince me that Bowen left me on that road without calling for help.

I know that where my father was concerned, there were still

inconsistencies with what really happened the night of the accident and following it. But who knew he'd still be wielding his torch of hate all these years later.

"Oh, he lost a baseball career that would probably have flamed out *anyway*. You were always too good for him, Lily, and that was demonstrated in the fact that even when he left you in the hospital, when he wouldn't return your letters or calls, you still forgave him. I don't see why you would be seeking affection from that scared little boy again."

He says all of this in a jovial way, as if his point is the most accurate and most obvious.

Mom's eyes narrow in his direction, but he just tucks into his plate of leftovers and begins to check his phone. "Eric, what has gotten into you? The girl hasn't laid eyes on a man in over ten years, don't you think there is a reason for that? This is a good thing."

They're speaking about me as if I'm not here, and suddenly, I'm seven again. No, not again. I've always been this obedient, insignificant thing that they can place in one spot and demand it do things. *Smile, don't speak unless spoken to, be home by curfew, no elbows on the table, dance with this advisor, don't date this boy, stay at home instead of moving out.*

All of it rushes at me at once, and I fly out of my seat. Before I know what's happening, my finger is in my father's face.

"How *dare* you! Talking about Bowen in that way ... it's slanderous. He is a good man."

I can't seem to summon all the words I would use to describe Bowen's goodness, because there are simply too many. And something tells me they'd be lost on my father.

He blinks up at me, his eyes actually resembling the father's I once knew. "Sweetheart, I'm simply trying to protect you. The Nash boys ... they seem to find themselves in trouble. First with your car accident, and that younger one with those meth dealers. The other one is in trouble with the law for hacking or coding or whatever it is. I simply don't want you getting mixed up in these things. You're too wonderful of a woman to give anything else to that riffraff."

My mouth hangs open. "I ... I don't even know what to say to that, other than you're wrong. And when I do eventually bring him over here for dinner, at Mom's request, I *won't* tell him all the horrible things you've said about him! He doesn't deserve to know the lies you've told me about him."

My father just scrolls through his phone, not bothering to look up as he sneers. "Don't bother, it won't last long enough for your mother to cook him a meal."

The chair scrapes the tile as I thrust it backward, and I'm in my car pulling out of the driveway before the tears even dare to form.

27

LILY

Lily: *I'm almost done here, just have to write up my assessment of the fourth-grade project I was helping the elementary school with. Want to grab dinner?*

I send the text in hopes that Bowen will say sure, and suggest Carlucci's, the only Italian restaurant in Fawn Hill. I've been stewing for days over what Penelope and Presley said about laying down the law with him when it comes to our relationship and where it's going. And ever since my father lit the match, I've begun to burn with the tension this issue is causing in my mind and heart.

If we're together, we should be together. No more not talking about what we're doing ... because we've been doing that all summer. And now summer is over. No more only seeing each other behind the closed doors of our homes. I want to be wooed; I want to date Bowen. As shallow and stupid as it sounds, I want to be seen about town with him. If not to quiet the rumors of our breakup so many years ago, then to show off how much *I* love *him*.

Bowen: *Sorry, late customer here at the shop. Then need to head home. Maybe you can come over later?*

And there it is again. This is the third time I've asked to go out for a meal, twice for dinner and once for brunch, that he's turned me down. Now it's becoming a pattern. And the fact that he turned it into me coming over to his place later ... it makes me feel cheap and hidden. Like a booty call or a woman he is ashamed of being seen with in public.

Lily: *No, if I go home, I'm in for the night. Guess I'll see you another time.*

My response is a little bit petulant, but a whole lot honest. I mean it; if he doesn't want to share a public meal together, then I'm not driving over to his house after ten p.m. to take off my clothes and sleep in his bed. My friends are right ... I'm not going to settle for being a good-time girl when Bowen had never treated me that way before. Just because we're adults now, and the way we define relationships might be murkier in this day and age, doesn't mean I'm going to agree to something I don't want.

Because what do I want? I want love and commitment, eventually marriage and a family. I want those things with Bowen, and we've fought through hell and back to even stand in the same room together let alone sleep together. It would be a shame if our generation's ridiculous dating pitfalls were the thing that ended us for good, but I'm willing to let them if he isn't willing to commit.

Bowen: *Sorry, baby. Working late. And I just want you to myself.*
Lily: *Those are bogus excuses. We both know it. I want to go out*

to eat with you. If you don't want to do that, then I have no problem going home alone.

He hit me with the baby ... probably as a cover-up tactic because he knows how much it melts me. But I'm not falling for it.

Texting always makes it easier to say how we truly feel because you're not standing right in front of that person. You're venting all of your frustrations at a screen, writing them out instead of having to articulate them in real time. It's both a pro and a con, because I know that I say things I wouldn't be bold enough to say to Bowen in person. But it also can't be read in the tone of voice I mean it in, so he is probably fuming at my attitude on the other end of the messages.

When I don't see a response for a few minutes, I put my phone down with a sigh. My hopes were up, and now they're dashed. I have that awful, rejected woman feeling in my stomach that can only be cured with a sleeve of Oreos and some caramel ice cream.

The last couple of studiers and readers shift their books around on their individual tables. The library closes at eight p.m. every weeknight, and it's almost seven thirty, so in about twenty minutes I get to ring the last call bell. While I love my job, those chimes always sound like freedom. I'm the sole full-time employee in my building, with a few part-timers that come and go during the week. But I open in the morning and lock up at night. I am responsible for its management, every project we partner with the schools on, every reading circle and book club ... all of it. When eight p.m. comes around, I'm exhausted and drained ... and just ready to snuggle under my covers with my latest read.

I put away the cart full of books that have been returned throughout the day. An encyclopedia in the research section, a couple of British history anthologies, several children's books and a random assortment of fiction.

By the time I make my way to the front, only two people are left sitting at tables, and it's almost time to ring the bell.

"Oh, I hope I didn't catch you on your way out. I need to check out a book."

A deep voice comes from the entryway to the library where the double doors still stand open. I recognize it, and immediately, my heart beats double time.

"What are you doing here?" I turn, Bowen's large, muscular frame coming into view.

He moves with grace and strength, my eyes combing his body from toes to hair as he comes to a stop in front of the big round help desk I stand behind. The dark stubble on his chin is shorter than it was when I saw him two days ago, and his ocean-colored eyes dance with amusement.

"I told you, I need to check out a book." The charming, crooked smile he's flashing at me holds hints of apologies.

My guard comes up, remembering that he's the one who just blew me off for dinner. "Thought you were busy."

"I wanted to come see my girl at work. Let it be known that I love books just as much as she does." He waggles his eyebrows and then winks.

Then it dawns on my slow, overtired brain. He came here tonight to show up for me. There may only be two people left in this library besides us, but technically, it's still public. Those two people see that Bowen Nash came to flirt with Lily Grantham at the library checkout desk ... they're here to witness it. Bowen is making an effort, because he could sense how upset I was about him shooting me down for dinner.

"Thank you for coming." I nod, trying to mask the emotion I feel from his gesture.

Bowen sighs, reaching for my hand. He lifts it to his lips, and doesn't kiss it, but simply rubs his mouth across my skin. The flesh he nuzzles simmers with heat that then travels all the way up my arm and suffuses my entire body.

"Baby, I'm sorry. I didn't mean to blow you off, or make it seem like I don't want to take you out." His fingers lace through mine as our hands lay together on the counter.

He's laying that charm on thick, and I see a glimpse of that boy I fell in love with. The one who saw something he wanted and went after it with brutal beguilement. Bowen is captivating, enchanting in this state, and it's hard to stay mad at him.

I purse my lips, trying to keep up the charade of my attitude. "I guess I can let you off the hook this time. But only because you came all the way across town to visit me at work."

As if that's really a trek. It's only about five minutes from his barbershop to the library, but I suppose he did close up quickly to come over here and apologize.

"You're too good to me. How much longer you got?" He taps his fingers on the counter, and I fixate on his thick, callused fingers. Gosh, I need to keep it together, there are still people in here. Maybe this is why we don't go out in public … I have ten years of unanswered lust to catch up on.

Glancing at the clock, I realize it's five minutes past when I was supposed to ring the last call bell. Without answering him, I hit the silver circle on top of the old-fashioned alert system on the counter and announce to the two patrons that it is seven fifty-five and we'll be closing in five minutes. They look up, pulled from their thoughts, and both begin to pack their bags and/or fold their laptops and store them away. The college-aged girl brings the three textbooks she was using up to the counter, and I smile and nod a thank you. The boy, who can't be much older than a freshman in high school, leaves his two books on the table before walking out.

I roll my eyes because someone needs to teach that boy

manners but I'm too drained for it tonight and go to collect those last two books. As Bowen roams the library, I go through the lockup procedures. Unlock the mechanisms that hold the entry doors open, close and lock from the inside. Shut down all the computers and turn off the lights from the back of the stacks to the front. Send the report of all the checked out books and overdue ones to the server and back it up before turning off my office computer for the night. Grab my coat and bag, lock my office, and then head out the employee entrance.

However, there is still a gorgeous man roving my library, and so I go in search of him.

I find him in one of the darkened stacks toward the middle of the room.

"You know, I probably haven't stepped foot in here since the research project I had to do at the beginning of senior year." Bowen has a book whose title I can't make out in his hand.

I set my coat and bag down on a table and join him in the shelves. "Is that because you were avoiding my turf, or reading in general?"

His eyes are sheepish when he turns them to me and shrugs. "Probably both."

"At least you're honest." I chuckle.

"Then know it's the truth when I tell you that you give sexy librarian a whole new definition."

Bowen gently drags me toward him, closing the small distance between us as his lips find mine. Is this what I wanted from the moment he walked into my library? Does it make me a shameless fool to answer yes? Just an hour ago, I was pouting because he wouldn't take me out to dinner and only wanted to have me come over to his house late at night. I'd taken a stand, and then he'd gotten me in the stacks and I'm melting like warm, gooey chocolate through his hands.

Talk about predictable.

But, I can't help it. Bowen's tongue is leading mine in a dance only we know the steps to, and each time I inhale, the scent of his musky cologne and old, weathered book pages is mixing and giving me one orgasmic arousal.

He turns us, my back hitting the metal shelf and rattling the thing all the way from the floor to the ceiling. Thick fingers tangle in my hair, and I cup his jaw in my hands, loving the rough tickle of the stubble beneath.

"I may not have stepped foot in here in ages, but I've had many fantasies about getting you between these stacks. There is something so naughty about making out in a library."

Bowen's whispers shoot straight from where he's sucking on my earlobe down to the middle of my thighs, drenching me.

"Have you thought about me touching you here?" he continues, his hand bunching my skirt and snaking under it.

I'm not sure if he means touching me in the library, or where his fingers currently push aside my underwear, but either way, I nod my head.

"All these long nights, you've probably thought about me pushing you up against all these books." Bowen's fingers demonstrate, penetrating me and I groan from the fullness.

My hands travel up and under the long sleeve tee he's wearing, tangling in the smattering of hair that gets thicker the farther down his happy trail I travel.

"More than I want to admit." My lips find the side of his neck.

In reality, I know we can't get caught. Only two other people have keys to this building, and they're not coming here at eight p.m. on a Wednesday. But just the fact that we're getting physical in my place of work is a huge turn on … one I'd fantasized about but never thought would happen.

"And you wanted me to take you to dinner? This is definitely more fun." He flashes me that cocky, younger-Bowen smile.

"Hmm ... I guess." A sly smile paints my lips. "But I'm not letting you off the hook for long. Especially since my mother wants to have you over for dinner." I chuckle into his neck.

Probably not the time to mention my mother, but he's making me weak and loopy, and I'm rambling.

Bowen's fingers stop stroking inside me, and he stills.

"You're telling people about us?" His voice takes on a hard edge.

I try to straighten where I've slouched against the shelves, doubt creeping up my neck in a heated blush. "Well, uh ... yes? I ... people saw us at the wedding and she asked me the other day ..."

I trail off, waiting for him to say it's fine and that he is glad we aren't hiding anymore. To continue building my climax.

But instead, Bowen is dead silent.

28

BOWEN

"Why would you tell her about us? We ... we haven't even talked about what we are."

When I pull back, the hurt in Lily's eyes is so clear, it's nearly blinding.

I probably just stuck my foot in my mouth, and I don't mean to be a complete asshole, but I'm panicking. If her mother knows about us ... fuck, then the senator definitely does. And I know explicitly what kind of lengths he'll go to, to keep me away from his daughter.

Lily's head snaps back a little, almost as if she'd been smacked. "What are you saying? Maybe we should talk about what we are because, clearly, we aren't on the same page."

She disengages herself from me, shoving my hand out from beneath her skirt and smoothing her clothes and hair before walking out of the stacks. I follow her, watch as she shrugs into her coat and slings her bag over her arm.

"Lily, I just don't want a lot of people finding out about us."

A sharp gasp comes from her, and I see the tears she's trying to blink back. "Well, talk about a one-eighty. I'm such an idiot."

Fuck. That came out wrong. What I mean, which I can't seem to say to her, is that I don't need the town gossiping about us. I guess I was the one who gave them all the ammunition they needed at the wedding. I was stupid for making out with Lily at the venue, for grinding up on her on the dance floor. But I'd been drunk off whiskey and high on the celebration of the day, and I'd been in love with the woman since I was sixteen. I wanted one night of freedom with her.

And now it was biting me in the ass. Because Lily took that as our coming out party. She'd probably talked to Presley and Penelope about us, if I had to guess, and she'd confirmed that her mother had heard about us. Which meant that most of the residents of Fawn Hill knew we were at least hooking up.

If I'm being honest, the other reason I don't want to have this talk with Lily, about *defining us*, is because once we do, it becomes real. We have to deal with all the real life shit we've been avoiding the past few months. Her texts before ... I thought that by coming over and showing up at her work, in public, that it would assuage her. Clearly, she'd been stewing over this more than she let on.

"That's not what I meant. I just ... I don't want to rush things. Getting parents involved, going out to dinner ... it means people in our business."

Lily throws up her hands, her bag weighing her arm down. "Maybe I want people in our business! Because gossip and public outings and all of our mutual friends asking questions ... it means we're real! Not just two people who sneak into each other's houses or hotel rooms. I'm not that girl, Bowen, and I think you know that."

She pauses, and I know she probably wants me to take what I've said back, or apologize, but I'm too confused right now. Surely, I know Lily is not that girl ... but she also doesn't know or understand a lot of what happened to separate us in the first place.

Because I haven't told her.

"We're not children, I'm not going to have a temper tantrum. But I'm also not not going to do this with you forever, Bowen. Not even for much longer. So make up your mind."

The rest of the week is dismal and depressing, with rain flooding out a lot of roads around Fawn Hill.

Business is slow, and I have too much time to think. My brothers end up coming over on Thursday and distracting me during the prime-time football game, but I'm glib and annoyed, leading them to taunt me even more.

I've worked myself into such a funk by Friday afternoon that I sound ticked off when I pick up the call coming into my cell from an unknown number.

"Yeah, who is this?" My voice is clipped and irritated.

"I'm calling for Bowen Nash? This is Daniel Ferapo with the St. Louis Tigers."

I perk up from where I'd been lounging on my couch, flipping through channels and not really watching. "Oh, yes, hello. This is Bowen.

A pause, and uncertainty in the man's voice. "We're the triple-A team out here ... I, uh, got your name from Lewis Mider. He said you were interested in getting back into the baseball industry. Have to say, I remember you as a high school ballplayer. You had a hell of an arm, Bowen."

The compliment stings more than it makes me shrug of modesty. Because he's right, I did have a hell of an arm. One that was crushed between the metal wreckage of my pickup ten years ago.

"Had a hell of a bat, too, but who's counting?" I crack the joke as if my heart doesn't rip the age-old stitches sewing it up.

Daniel chuckles on the other end of the phone. "Can't argue with that. Listen, we're interviewing for an assistant hitting coach position, and Lewis told me you might be looking for something just like that. Do you have some time to talk about it?"

Christ, I'd just walked right into an interview without even knowing it. The least Lewis could've done was give me a heads-up, but maybe he hadn't known Daniel was going to call me. Either way, I scramble, looking around for a notebook or something. The best I come up with is the envelope for my last cable bill and a half-sharpened pencil.

"Sure, thank you for giving me a call. I'd love to discuss the position."

Over the next half hour, I try my best to fake it through this interview as professionally as I can. Of course, I know all the baseball terminology and statistics, but I wasn't prepared for some of Daniel's questions. Such as, how I thought their season had gone this year. Well ... I wouldn't know that since I had no time to do any research before their general manager called me. And he asked some pointed questions about how I thought the farm systems should be structured and what changes needed to be implemented. Unfortunately, I'd been out of that world for a long time and hadn't stayed current with the politics going on inside any league beyond the majors. I fumbled my way through those questions while giving some great insight on others.

The hardest question he lobbed at me was one he probably thought was a softball. But asking where I saw myself in five years? That was a complete mindfuck.

I could be anywhere. St. Louis. Another farm team. Fawn Hill, with Lily by my side.

All in all, the interview was probably a mixed bag, and I came out of it feeling winded but proud of myself for being able to hang on through it.

Right now, I'm not sure where my head is at. I could be on a plane to St. Louis before I know it, with a chance at a fresh start.

But leaving Fawn Hill? I guess I'd never thought about it seriously. As a kid, it was a far-off dream that I'd go to the major leagues. I'd never really thought about the semantics of leaving my hometown. And even though I sought possible positions in baseball and out, I'd never considered the full ramifications of what they'd bring. Which was leaving behind everything and everyone I knew and loved.

My head was running in a million different directions, and who knew if I'd even get this position. Or any other.

But I did know where my heart was at, and it had a lot of apologizing to do.

29

LILY

I'm a stupid, *stupid* woman.

Who almost slipped up and told the man who didn't even want to take her out in public that she was in love with him.

That she had been in love with him since the day she'd laid eyes on him, and it had stayed that way for the ten years he'd abandoned her.

I beat myself up for a week about what happened in the library. And the worst part is, I think about it all day at work because that's where the ultimatum happened. The library is my safe haven, the place I go to escape all the stress in my life. But the past week, all I think about when I look around my domain is Bowen, pushing me up against the stacks and kissing the rational thought out of me.

Having had the Mondayest Monday in the history of Mondays, I decide that I've earned a nice, long soak in the bath with a glass of wine as I pull into my driveway.

Grabbing the mail out of the box next to my doorbell, I twist the key in the lock and my shoulders sag as I walk into the space where I can be fully alone.

That's when the scene in front of me hits my eyes.

Lilies. *Hundreds* of them, covering my first floor. On every surface, littering my couches, petals sprinkled on the floor.

My home smells like a greenhouse, one of those big, beautiful glass domes that contain every flower known to man. Every single color pops in my vision, and I want to cry it's so pretty. Beautiful, is the word I'm looking for ... there is something so beautiful about a fresh, blossomed flower. Something that strikes a deep chord inside a person, especially me. Rationally, I know that flowers are a plant and they're put on earth to perpetuate the life cycle and eco-system. But to me? They're here to bring the simplest form of joy ... to brighten your day.

I told Bowen as much the first time he bought a corsage for me. It had been full of purple and white lilies and fastened with a pearl bracelet.

That's how I know that this gesture is from *him*. That this is his apology.

It's how I know he's feeling just as disconnected and awful as I am about not seeing each other for the past week.

Walking through the first floor, I marvel at all the gorgeous blooms.

"How ...?" I trail off, asking no one in particular how the heck he pulled this off.

It's at this exact moment that my doorbell rings.

Running through the hall, I skid to a stop in front of the door and wrench it open.

I know I probably have a silly smile on my face, and my cheeks are pink from blushing and running. And that I should be more stern with Bowen in this moment, make him work for it.

But I just can't. Not with all these lilies around me.

"I'm sorry." Bowen stands in my doorway in dark black jeans and a black leather jacket.

And in his outstretched hand, he holds one beautiful, full-blossomed, purple lily.

It takes every ounce of strength in me not to fling myself at him and sob tears of joy like a hysterical damsel. Instead, I stand there, open-mouthed, unable to form words.

"I should have never said those things to you. I should have never treated you that way. You were right, you shouldn't have to settle for the attention of a man who is half in. You are the ultimate catch, Lily, and I've always known that. It just took a sharp slap to the brain to make me remember it. And I don't want to catch you, I want *you* to pick *me*. I want to be the man worthy enough of you ... and after our history, part of me was afraid to be that man. But I'm not anymore. I'm in love with you, Lily."

My brain short circuits. Did he just say he loves me? "What?"

"I love you. I've loved you since the minute I saw you. Hell, probably even before then. I love you so deeply, that when I'm not with you, my bones ache. I've been dead inside for the last ten years, and the only thing that's kept me going are the glimpses I catch of you. I am in love with you. I'm in this. Completely."

Now I do jump into his arms and surrender to the hysterics. Just like a damsel.

Bowen catches me, our lips meeting at the exact moment our bodies collide. I can taste the salt of my tears as I kiss him, and I'm blubbering as we make up.

"I'll tell anyone you want me to that I love you. I'll run into Kip's during the breakfast rush and shout it out loud." Bowen sets me down, backing me into my foyer.

I chuckle against his mouth. "I think that might be overkill. I'd settle for the lunch rush, though."

"Deal," he murmurs, tucking the single lily behind my ear.

Collecting myself, as much as a woman assaulted with so

much love can, I stare up at him dreamily. "How did you even get all these into my place?"

Bowen winks. "A magician never reveals his secrets."

"Presley gave you her key, didn't she?"

He shrugs. "She may have."

We both laugh. I can't stop staring at him, at how rugged and handsome he looks in the middle of all these pretty flowers.

"I love you, too, you know." The minute the words leave my lips, a weight lifts off my heart. "I've been waiting a long time to tell you that, again."

Bowen takes my face between his hands, those turquoise eyes searing into mine. "Never stop saying it, ever again."

"So, I know I said I wanted you to take me out, and not just come over late ... but now that we're here ..."

It could be his all-black attire that's making me feel like the wild teen he once turned me into. It could be the dozens and dozens of flowers blossoming on my first floor. Or it could just be that Bowen Nash has the magnetism of every species in the animal kingdom, he's that drop-dead hunky.

Because right now, I really want him in my bed, naked.

"Oh, you didn't think this apology came with makeup sex, did you?" Bowen smirks. "Because I was just going to kiss you good night and go home."

"Were you?" My fingers work to unzip the back of my dress, the sound echoing off the wall and causing heat to pool in Bowen's eyes.

He licks his lips. "Yeah, okay, you convinced me. Make-up sex sounds like the best way to seal this deal."

A breathy laugh escapes my lips as he lunges for me, hauling me up and over his shoulder to go in search of my bedroom.

While Bowen's apology and the make-up sex we were about to bring the house down with are sincere, there is still that niggling feeling of doubt in the back of my mind. I try to push it away, lock it up for another time, but it's still there, itching at me like a newly healed scab.

He still hasn't explained his ten-year distance. I know that, eventually, we'll have to talk about it. That just like not settling for the booty call label, I also won't settle for his excuse of not being able to tell me. I won't be able to settle for not knowing the entire truth.

But tonight, I'm letting myself be carried away, literally. By Bowen, by the flowers, by the declaration of love. Because I deserve it. *We* deserve it.

It's been too long since the purest form of love existed in my life, and I'm taking it at face value tonight.

30

BOWEN

Main Street is aglow with the flicker of its real gas street lamps as the first cool night of fall has Lily shivering in her sweater.

"I should have brought a real coat. But I wanted to keep denying it was really moving into the winter months."

I shrug out of my leather jacket and wrap it around her shoulders. "That's the kind of thinking that will help you catch pneumonia."

"But it's a good thing my boyfriend has a jacket to warm me with." She smiles up at me, and I fake shiver in my button-down.

Lily laughs as we walk up to Carlucci's, the nicest restaurant in Fawn Hill. It wasn't much, no crystal stemware or wine by the bottle, but their marinara sauce was out of this world and the service was excellent. The family who owned it were also good friends of my parents, and both Lily and I had come here plenty of times growing up.

Taking her to dinner was a risk I was willing to take. There was a real possibility that Eric Grantham would begin his crusade to ruin me like he'd promised if he ever found out I was sniffing around his daughter again. But ... after spending so much time with Lily, I almost didn't care anymore. I was a grown man, no longer a little boy quaking in my boots at the thought of what my father or her father might do to us if we didn't stay apart.

I'd told her I was in love with her, and that was blinding me. It made me feel invincible, especially since she'd said it back, and that numbing agent was either great or disastrous. Senator Grantham, in all likelihood, already knew about us. But, it was a necessary evil I'd have to combat. I was in a relationship with Lily now, and that meant public outings. That meant showing other people how I felt about her.

If he wanted to come after me, I wasn't going down without a fight. And in the meantime, I was going to live my life. Shit, it had been ten years since I'd really lived the way I wanted to.

As we walked up to Carlucci's, a familiar figure lingers by the entrance, holding what appears to be a bottle of wine.

"Mrs. Nash?" Lily cocks her head to the side, a curious smile painting her blood-red lips.

She's never worn the color on her mouth before, and it's driving me a little insane. I want to feast on it, kiss it right off.

"Lily! Oh, I am so glad Bowen asked me to come tonight. I've been waiting, rather impatiently, for our reunion. And how many times have I told you, call me Eliza!"

My mother wraps Lily up in a hug, and the two women embrace as if one is a soldier coming home from war. Lily pulls back and smiles at me while giving me a look that says, "Wow, you're taking me to dinner with your Mom. I'm impressed."

Taking her to dinner with my mother? That just shows her how serious I am about her. Or so I hope it will. My mother adores Lily, always has, and she was practically giddy when I told her that we were officially dating again and I wanted to take them both to Carlucci's.

"Shall we?" I open the door, letting them pass through.

Once inside, Mom greets Mr. Carlucci at the host stand with a double cheek kiss, and Lily gets one, too. I shake his hand, and from there we're escorted to our table. As we peruse the menu which we've all had memorized for about twenty years, my mother asks Lily how the library is. She used to volunteer there every month or so but was asked to be a school lunch aide this year and has given herself fully to the task. Mom loves children and getting to supervise the elementary school kids each day is the highlight of her life right now.

I listen as they chatter back and forth about the town, Mom's new job, the projects Lily has going on, the upcoming holidays, and everything in between. I just sit back, contributing to the conversation every now and then, but genuinely happy to hear the two most important women in my life get along.

Some restaurant patrons are looking at us, trying to be discreet about it but I can still feel their eyes. I purposely hook my arm around Lily's shoulders as we sit side by side, so everyone knows that yes, they're finally together. Bowen Nash and Lily Grantham have finally squashed their beef and are in love again. I wouldn't be surprised if it was a story in the paper next week, that's how weirdly obsessed this town was with its gossip.

"Bowen, have you heard anything back from that team in St. Louis?" Mom asks, dipping a piece of crusty bread into the sauce on her pasta dish.

I nearly choke on the sip of wine I just swallowed. Jesus, she just lobbed that grenade out of left field.

"Ah, no, I haven't heard anything." I wipe my mouth with my napkin, trying to downplay this whole topic of conversation.

"Well, I think it's so great that you want to try to get back into baseball." Mom claps her hands together.

She has no idea how awkward she just made this dinner but bless her for being a wonderful mother who supports me.

"You want to play again?" Lily looks me in the eye, her voice taking on an uncertain note.

I shrug, fumbling to explain. "Well, no. Coach, probably. Or scout. Or nothing. I don't know, I just thought ... before we got back together I put some feelers out there. That's all."

Lily nods. "And you had an interview?"

Mom cuts in. "With a minor league team in Missouri. For a hitting coach position. Don't you remember how great he was out on that field?"

The smile that crosses my mom's face is one of pride, and it must be contagious because Lily takes on the same expression.

"I do. Remember when he hit that grand slam in the playoffs junior year?" She grins up at me.

My mother nods, laughing. "And his face was so smug as he rounded those bases. That was off that pitcher who'd been throwing insults at him on social media before the game."

"Cracked my lucky bat in half, but it had been worth it." I chuckled, somewhat surprised at how light this conversation is.

Typically, when I think about my glory years on the diamond, it's shaded with bitterness and regret.

But tonight, I'm ... having *fun* remembering the old days.

The rest of dinner goes off without a hitch and leaves us all with smiles on our faces and holding our very full stomachs. When Mr. Carlucci comes over asking if we'd like dessert, we all beg off after having stuffed ourselves with pasta and bread. I pick up the bill like the gentleman I am who is trying to impress both his mother and his girlfriend. And when Mr. Carlucci comes back with my card, he drops off two takeout bags of hot, gooey chocolate chip cookies.

After kissing my mother goodbye and making sure she gets to her car safely, Lily and I head home.

Ten minutes later, as we walk into my house, the topic I've been trying to shy away from is at the forefront of Lily's mind.

"So, you had an interview?" Lily's trying to be curious, but I know she is hurt that I didn't tell her about my job search.

Or explain what it might mean for us.

"It was unexpected. Honestly, it wasn't even scheduled. I spoke with one scout I used to know, and he sent them my way. I probably won't even get it. I'm not even sure I want it."

I'm rambling, which is so unlike me, and Lily hasn't turned to look at me since we walked through the front door.

"Okay. Well, just ... keep me in the loop, okay?"

Her voice has a forced lightness to it, and I know I should reassure her, be honest about what my intentions were when I took that interview ... but I don't want to get into it. Just like every other serious issue plaguing our relationship, I push it to the back for just a little while longer.

I nod, crossing to her to take her coat and hang it on the rack.

"Now, let's dig into that bag of cookies. Better yet, let's take them to bed." She smiles, reaching for the takeout bag Mr. Carlucci left with our check.

Thank God she is letting this drop for now. I don't think I have another fight left in me after the past week of tension with her, and I am being honest. Even if I was offered the position, I'm not sure I'd take it.

Twenty-five minutes later, we're both in bed, Lily's face is washed and free of the minimal makeup she wears, and there are chocolate chip cookie crumbs dotting the sheets.

It's then that she asks me the hardest question she has about the accident, yet she has no idea it's the most difficult to answer.

"Do you miss him? Your father?" Lily looks up at me, her eyes so innocent. "Being at dinner tonight with your mother, I could feel his presence. It must be very hard for her. For all of you."

How do I answer that question? Of course, I miss my dad.

His death is the second most horrible thing I've ever experienced, the first being our accident. It's a specific kind of torture, losing a parent. Especially for a son to lose his father. I feel like I've become untethered like there was this person who anchored me and now I have to make every decision without consulting that source of solidness. There was grief, hurt, anger at him leaving so soon and then there was something else.

Since the day my father had come to me and said stay away from Lily, I'd hated him. A part of me smoldered with the fury I held like a torch for him, and it hadn't abated to this day. His death had only intensified the feeling because we'd never resolved any of it. The day he revealed the mutually assured destruction pact to me, I'd been so angry that I'd barely spoken to him for months afterward.

On the outside, our relationship may have thawed. But really, I'd always carried this resentment. And now it had nowhere to go, except fester inside me like an old, infected wound.

So instead of being honest, I lie. I tell her what she wants to hear. "Of course. Every day."

Lily sighs. "I'm sorry I couldn't be there for you."

My brow furrows. "You were at the funeral."

I remember seeing her there, in her black dress. Even in black, even though we were standing across the room at my father's funeral, I remember thinking how beautiful she looked. And then an idea had sprung ... since my father was dead, I no longer had to stay away from her.

My feet had begun dragging me to her, one step across the church and then the next ...

Until I saw Senator Grantham pull her into his side. He was the only person smirking at my father's funeral mass, and the grin was directed right at me.

He knew that I knew about the deal they'd struck. And it was clear, from his expression, that he expected me to abide by the rules even after my father's passing. It made that day even harder than it should have been.

"I know." Lily sighs, breaking me from those thoughts. "I just mean, I wish I could have *been* there for you. I ... these last ten years have been so hard. With no explanation, we were separated for ten years ..."

She still wants me to explain why I left her in the hospital. And we're wading into dangerous territory again. "Lily ..."

"I know. *I know*. But come on, Bowen, I can't just take 'I can't tell you that' as an answer forever. I can't lie here, in your bed, pretending that after a decade of heartache and pain, we're just completely fine again. We've taken it slow, and now we're in deep. At least I am. Aren't you?"

Gently, I lay my lips on her cheek. "I took you to dinner with my mother tonight. At Carlucci's, in front of the whole town. You know me, and I'm not a public guy. I'd say that should show you just how all in I am with you. And don't give me this whole, 'aren't you?' question. I told you, and I'll keep telling you, I'm in love with you. As deep and as wide as the ocean, baby."

I know I'm trying to make light of the situation, but part of me wants to delay the inevitable for a little longer. We just got on solid ground, having told each other our true feelings.

She gently nudges my shoulder with her hand. "I love you, too. But don't make a joke out of this. I know we're good, but I want to be exceptional. I want to have a relationship with no secrets, one where we can acknowledge our past but feel no bitterness toward it."

Obviously, this gorgeous woman in bed next to me is right, but I just can't tell her yet. I need a little while longer where she doesn't look at me with betrayal and hurt in her eyes.

Because that's how she will look at me.

"We've had a nice night. I know you deserve an answer, but

can we just take it one hurdle at a time? We said I love you. We went out on a date, which also happened to reconnect you and my mother. Can that be enough for tonight?"

Please, God, let it be enough.

When Lily leans over to plant a kiss on my lip, then turns her light out, I know I'm off the hook for one more night.

"I love you," she whispers into the darkness, curling her body against mine.

It takes me a full hour and a half staring off at the ceiling before my worried brain finally gives out and allows me to fall asleep.

31

LILY

Presley and I roll up our yoga mats, the sweat on mine leaving me semi-disgusted.

"We should probably put an ambulance on standby next time we decide to do hot yoga by ourselves." She opens the front door of the studio and a cold gust of October wind flies in.

I breathe the frigidity in and chuckle. "Imagine? Us passed out on the floor because we wanted an intense workout."

"I've seen crazier at a soul cycle class." Presley laughs, handing me a cup of strawberry-infused water as she fills one for herself.

Breathing in through my nose, I try to calm my racing heart down after the yoga boot camp my friend just put me through. She's testing out classes to add to the schedule, and apparently, I'm her guinea pig. Not that I mind ... it means a free class and a crazy good workout.

"Your customers are going to love that class. I feel like I just ran a marathon in a sauna. I may not need to work out for the next week."

Presley shakes her head. "No, we want people to come back every day. That's the whole point of business."

As if she needs to worry about that. The studio is doing great and is the talk of the town. Even most of the older crowd in Fawn Hill love Presley's senior classes on Tuesday and Thursday mornings.

"So business is doing great, but how about you and your husband?" I wink, calling Keaton by his new moniker.

She blushes. "Isn't it so sexy that he's my husband? Who would have thought, me, gushing over the title of the man in my life?"

"I did. From the minute I saw you two together the first time, I knew it was meant to be." I smugly nod my head.

Presley rolls her eyes, sitting on one of the chairs near the front door to put her sneakers on. "You wear such rose-colored glasses, Lil. I love that about you."

Something about her words snag on my heart. "And sometimes it gets me into trouble."

My friend looks up, surveying my expression. "Uh oh, what's going on?"

I shrug, doing that fake thing people do when they act like they don't want to talk about it, but really they want to.

Presley catches on. "Don't tell me nothing. Your shoulders sagged with relief when I asked what was wrong, so spill. You forget that I teach yoga for a living. It's literally my job to read the areas in people's bodies where they carry stress."

"You're right ... and of course, it's Bowen. We went to dinner the other night with Eliza, which was wonderful. You're so lucky she is your mother-in-law."

"I know," Presley agrees, smiling.

I continue, "But she let slip that he is interviewing with minor league baseball teams for coaching positions. Teams in other states. Possibly even across the country. He didn't even tell me, Pres. I feel like every time I turn around, there is another secret he's been keeping. I hate that I'm being left in the dark."

Past the floor-to-ceiling windows that make up the shopfront of the studio, Main Street bustles with Saturday afternoon energy.

"I thought you were doing so great, though. He told you he loves you."

"He did. But he's also keeping secrets. About our past, about what's happening right under my nose. It's my fault as well. I keep letting him get away with this stuff. I know I do; I know I'm pulling the wool over my own eyes. But part of me wants to stay in this happy little bubble for a little while longer? We love each other, right? Can't that be enough for now?"

"It can, as long as you're not affected by or thinking about all of those issues on a daily basis." Presley's expression clues me in to the fact that she knows I'm always thinking about them.

And she's right. Because when I'm not with Bowen, pretending we don't have any elephants sitting in every room we occupy together, I'm always thinking about them. The elephants, the issues, whatever you want to call them ... they're always on my mind.

"How can he keep these things bottled up so tightly?"

Presley smiles. A small, sympathetic smile, one that says she's not saying what she really wants to.

"What?" My tone is all attitude.

She sighs. "Bowen is the middle child."

"He's one of four." Her math makes no sense.

"That may be, but Keaton is the oldest, which makes him the golden boy. Believe me, I'm married to the man. In the eyes of his family, he can do wrong. I kind of hate him for it sometimes. And the twins are a set, they're basically one giant baby and Eliza treats them as such. I love her, but the twins can also get away with murder and she won't bat an eye. Bowen, he's the middle child ... he's like me."

My heart settles, opening to listen to her. "What do you mean?"

"You'll never truly understand if you're not a middle child, and I love you as much as I love yoga, but you're an *only child*, Lil. You'll never really get what it's like to scrounge for attention, to try to live up to a sibling or appear the best in your parent's eyes. Or, when all that goes south, to just keep everything to yourself. It's a default for you, you get every role."

Presley goes on, "Bowen and I, we were the forgotten ones. I've never actually spoken to him about it, but I know that for me, being a middle child determined the way I blossomed. It dictated a path I followed for a long time, and only once I truly stopped caring what other people thought and had the unconditional love of someone who truly cared *for me*, was I able to veer off it. Naturally, my family loves me, as does Bowen's, but there were whole years where my parents spent more time on my brother and sister than me. I think ... not that Eliza meant to do it, but Bowen could have been in that position, too. It doesn't help that he's the introvert, that he literally doesn't like to be complimented or given praise. After the ... after your accident ended his career, he probably retreated further into that middle child role. It's tough, and you can't escape the loneliness of it sometimes. That's all I'm saying."

"So you think ... you think he's avoided me for so long because he's a middle child?" I'm confused now.

Presley rubs my shoulder. "That's not what I'm saying. I think he keeps his secrets, his thoughts, his choices, to himself because he grew up being the last one thought of. He's used to receiving less love, and it's sharpened him. It's also made him self-reliant. I know that's how I used to feel. Like if I got too close to having something I really wanted or talked about it too much, it would ruin it. That might not make any sense, and it could be completely wrong, but maybe that's what's been holding him back from really opening up."

Her words give me pause, and I chew my lip as I think it over. "But in my mind, that just doesn't add up. I've tried to get through to him so many times. We were so in love; we *are* in love …"

"And he blames himself for almost killing you. You didn't see yourself in that hospital bed. Imagine sitting next to his lifeless body for a month while machines breathed for him? That's gotta fuck with a person, Lil."

And that connects with me. Straight to my brain, a whack as hard as a baseball. I never really thought about how awful it must have been for Bowen. He'd been driving. For me, our accident was a split second. We flipped in the truck and then I woke up in a hospital bed. But for him …

It had been months of agony. Of healing himself and watching me for any flicker of life. Now that Presley said it, I couldn't imagine holding it together for that long if the roles had been reversed.

"And would it be so bad if Bowen took a job outside of Fawn Hill?" Presley asks cautiously.

The words smack me, bouncing off my head and disorienting me. "You're suggesting it would be a good thing if he left town? If he left me?"

She waves her hands above her head. "Gah! Hold up. Sorry, that thing happened where I think the rest of the sentence in my head but don't say it. What I meant was, it might be a good thing if he got a job offer, so you could both leave *together*."

This idea is even crazier and has me snorting. "Um, what are you even talking about? How did this go from me complaining about him keeping secrets, to Bowen's middle child status, to you telling me we need to hit the road?"

Presley nods. "I know, sometimes my train of thought can be

all over the place. But, hear me out. If Bowen did get a job with a team outside of the state, wouldn't that give you two a fresh start? You can work anywhere, Lily! Libraries exist all over the country. But imagine leaving Fawn Hill, which holds so many bad memories for you two, and moving somewhere that you can make all new ones?"

I'd never actually thought about leaving the town I grew up in. With a father in the public eye and my loyalty to my parents, it had never really been an option. It had always just been expected that I'd attend college nearby and then move back once I was done. Presley makes a valid point.

Maybe I shouldn't look at Bowen's silence as hiding things from me or keeping me in the dark. Perhaps, since we've been apart, this has just become his nature.

And maybe, just maybe, his behind-the-scenes plans will lead to something bigger and better for us.

32

BOWEN

The only other person I've ever leaked the secret about our father's deal to is Keaton.

One night, shortly after Dad's death, I'd been drowning in a half-empty bottle of vodka, hurting like hell from losing our father. And I needed someone to spill my darkest thoughts to.

He'd been stunned, understandably. That our father would do such a thing, that Eric Grantham would do such a thing. Keaton had wanted me to tell Lily right away, but he hadn't seen her father's display of pompousness at the funeral. That was a clear threat.

And now, I was too far gone. I needed him to remind me why I needed to stay away from her.

That's why I'm in his office, having brought him lunch from Kip's, to sweeten him up.

"I saw you at the wedding. You two are still those madly in love teenagers I used to roll my eyes at when you disappeared into the basement." Keaton rolls his eyes even now, taking a bite of his BLT.

We had some *good times* in that basement, Lily and me.

"That's the problem. It's ... we picked up right where we left off. We're together, full out and in public. That's dangerous, Keat."

"Why?"

"You know why."

"Because she might find out what you've been hiding from her? Because her father is a prick who's been threatening you and our family for years? Or because you're scared, that at the end of all this, you might have to face the thing you're really afraid of?"

That strikes a nerve. "And what is that?"

My hand smacks the top of his desk and ruffles the plate that contains the cheeseburger I haven't touched.

Keaton sighs. "Brother, I'm not trying to upset you. I'm trying to get to the root of the issue, and I'm going to shoot straight with you like I always have. You are in love with Lily. Always have been. And that love, it almost got her killed. You're so afraid of what will happen if you two can love each other freely, if you can end up together and happy, that it's scared you into not pursuing her at all. Or else you wouldn't be here, asking me to talk you out of being with her."

And there it is. The slice that cuts so deep, you can't even feel yourself bleeding until you're lying on the floor taking your last breath. Because my brother is absolutely right. All the other stuff that has kept me away from Lily? I've used it as my armor. Take that away, and I'd have to wrestle the real demon.

"You need to tell her, Bowen." Keaton folds his hands on his desk.

I get up, pacing around the office. "How am I supposed to do that? She'll hate me."

He shrugs. "That may be, but she deserves the truth. You love each other, you always have. If you tell her, maybe you can get through it together. But the time for lying is up."

I shake my head, muttering to myself. I've officially gone crazy. My double life has finally melted my brain to the point of insanity.

"Bowen, come on. It's been ten years. The situation you and Lily were in when you were in high school, those things don't even exist anymore. Think about it, what does Senator Grantham have against you? There are no more baseball prospects for you. I'm sorry, but it's true. You have nothing to lose in terms of your future because you're in it. You have an established barbershop, one that, honest to God, he would be wasting his time to take away from you. You also are a man in this community, one who has people who will rally behind me when push comes to shove. And Lily? She is a grown woman. No one is going to care that she unbuckled her seatbelt to go down on you."

I glare at him.

"They're not! Sure, it's a little scandalous, but people in this town have been on the edge of their seats forever to see you two get back together. If Grantham releases that secret about his own daughter, that her own recklessness was the reason she was ejected from the car, then he is a bigger prick than even you and I imagined. But if he does, that storm will blow over in a couple of days. The bigger news will be that childhood sweethearts found love again. So I ask you, what the hell do either of you have to lose anymore?"

That's when the epiphany happens. He's fucking right. So fucking right. I've been quaking in my boots for the last ten years ... for what? The futures we held back then are gone. The senator can't get to me anymore. Sure, he can make idle threats about coming for my family, but I'm not a boy anymore. I'm not David and he's not Goliath. I can take him on, and I've got more ferocity. I'd win. If he even cared to waste his time and try.

"Why do you always have to be so noble?" I seethe.

"Because I'm the big brother and your ugliest mirror. I show you what needs to be done, even if it isn't fun. And I think you mean that I'm right. Come on, tell me I'm right."

I ignore his demand. "Yeah, I'd call you the biggest killjoy I know."

"I'm okay with that. As long as you buck up and finally set things right."

It's going to hurt, but I know I have to do it.

33

BOWEN

"You're chopping it wrong."

Lily giggles as she walks over, putting her hand on top of mine to correct the way I'm cutting a red bell pepper.

"It's all going to be stuffed inside a taco shell, so who cares what shape it is?" I grumble.

"It'll taste better if you do it like this." She guides my hand.

I drop the knife, moving to attack her cheek with kisses instead. "I know how to make it taste the *best*."

Laughter bubbles up out of her throat as she swats me away, moving to the other side of the kitchen where she's browning the meat in a skillet. "I'm hungry and you're distracting me. Focus!"

We cook in contented silence, the way we have every night for almost two weeks. There is something to be said about having a woman, or a partner, in general, in your life, in your house. Everything feels ... warmer. I look forward to going home to her. Waking up in the morning, doing our early hours routine together, following her down the street before she turns one way and I turn the other ... it's all just *better* with her.

"Have you heard anything from St. Louis?"

And then Lily brings it all crashing down on my head with one simple question.

"No, still haven't heard." My voice is a mask of nonchalance.

"Hmm, okay. Is there anything else you might want to tell me about?"

She hasn't brought up the stuff we avoid talking about since we became exclusive. But I can tell she has a bee in her bonnet tonight, and that fucker is probably going to end up stinging me.

I sigh, frustrated. "Lil, it was a long time ago. I told you, I can't talk about it. What does it matter now?"

"It matters to me!" Her voice rises three octaves and I immediately know that my choice of words was wrong. "I still need to know why, Bowen. For ten years, you blatantly ignored me. You had me hating myself, wondering what I did wrong."

I slam the knife down on the cutting board, harder than I'd intended to. "We're so good now. Nothing can break us apart. Let's just leave the past in the past."

Keaton's voice echoes in my head. I should tell her. She's asking me to tell her. But something in me knows ... that if I do, it might just end us for good.

Lily takes a minute to collect herself, pinching the bridge of her nose and breathing deeply. "Bowen ... I know that you're used to keeping things to yourself. That you're quiet and usually go at life alone. I realize you've been operating this way for a long time, and I'm trying to be understanding, but we're a partnership now. I love you, and you can tell me anything. I want to know what you're thinking about, what's weighing on you."

If she knew what I knew, she wouldn't wish that. Ten minutes from now, she'll hate me. But she's worn me down, and she's right. I'm tired of carrying this secret, the big one, alone.

Breathing what feels like my last solid breath, I take a moment to memorize her face. In the loving expression it's in right now, gazing at me openly with those navy eyes and all the dark hair swirling around her elegant cheekbones and jaw.

"After the accident, I sat by your bedside for what felt like an eternity. Day in and day out, I prayed for you to wake up. And then one day, about a week before you actually did, my father came to me and told me I needed to stay away from you. My father and your father ... they made a pact. One that would ruin both you and I if we didn't break up. He told me that if we didn't end our relationship, your father was going to smear both our names. So I did. I left before I even knew if you were going to live, and I stayed away for ten years."

Lily drops the spatula she was using, her eyes glazing over with pain. "What ...?"

I cross the kitchen in a few strides, but Lily holds up her hand to stop me. She doesn't want me touching her. And that's how I realize there is no taking this back. My words are branded on our relationship now.

My voice is a begging plea. "Lily, listen, *please*. I was protecting you. That's all I was ever trying to do. I couldn't see a way out of it ... I was so damn scared that I caused your death, or what your father would do to you if you woke up. What he'd do to you because of me. So I decided to protect you. That's why I left. Why I stayed away, why I avoided you. It wasn't because I didn't love you. God, I love you so much. I let them manipulate me, let them drag me into their fucked-up little pact *because* I love you."

"You ... you lied to me." Lily's voice is shaking, and it matches the tremors working through her body.

I reach for her, but she wrenches her arm away. "No, baby, I ..."

"Don't *baby* me. You kept this horrible, enormous secret from me for ten years, Bowen! *Ten years*. Do you know what we could have solved together if you'd let me in on what our fathers had done? Do you even know that I wouldn't have cared what they'd promised to do to us?"

"Lily, do you remember how we crashed?" I stop her tirade in its tracks.

"Of course, I do." Her voice is hysterical.

"Your father, my father ... they were going to tell everyone why you unbuckled your seatbelt. Why you were ejected. I couldn't ... I couldn't let that happen. I didn't want you to feel any shame or any hurt from the accident. So I left. I cut out my own damn heart to save you."

Her eyes turn murderous. I'm about to hyperventilate. My system is malfunctioning, my heart beats too fast and I feel like I might pass out, throw up, or have a seizure all at the same time.

"I would have let my reputation go to hell and back, for all I cared. I just wanted you!" she screams.

Before I can even give my rebuttal, Lily is fleeing my kitchen and heading for the hallway. I should stop her, make her listen, try *anything* to get her to stay ...

But I know it's too late. I lost her when I walked out of that hospital room, and I'm losing her again because of the decision I made that day.

We are tarnished, our love is stained with the blood of my betrayal, of my lie. And there is no wiping us clean.

34

BOWEN

Living a life without Lily was, unfortunately, something I already knew how to do.

Going through each day with a titanium lock weighing down my heart, that's normal for me. I've carried this baggage on my shoulders for ten years. I know how to avoid her in town, calculate her movements so that I didn't show up in the same places, steel myself to seeing a glimpse of her hair or the strut of her legs.

I've walked around like a shell of myself for a decade plus ... and I guess it's back to that again.

I knew from the moment the words came out of my mouth; it could only end one way. Lily viewed my keeping the most enormous secret of my entire life from her as a betrayal rather than me protecting her. She thinks I lied to her for ten years and lumps me into the same category as our fathers. To her, I am the enemy because I didn't allow her to be a part of anything.

I can't blame her. I'm not even surprised that she hates me now. I hate me. I've hated me for ten years. For keeping quiet all this time, for letting my father persuade me to leave her, for staying away like a coward, in fear of her father for so long.

But the thing I hate the most? That I didn't get to tell her I love her for the last three thousand, six hundred and fifty odd days. I was the one who made us miss all that time, and now Lily knew that.

There was no way she was going to forgive me.

And because of that, I had a decision to make.

I'd heard from Daniel, the general manager of the team in St. Louis, two days after our blowout fight at my house. And while I might have heard from him, the person I wanted most to call still hadn't. Lily was dodging my calls, texts, and either wouldn't answer the door or wasn't home the two times I stood on her stoop with flowers. She was icing me out. Either that ... or she had nothing left to say.

Daniel did though. He told me that the other coaches were familiar with my baseball stats in high school and that while they were wary about my lack of coaching or work in the industry, they wanted to give me a try.

That's right ... I was offered the position. I'm honestly a little shocked, still, that he wants to hire me. I never thought that initial phone call would turn out this way, and now that it has ...

I really don't know what to do. The possibility of leaving Fawn Hill was never real until it was. I'd have to sell my shop and my house. I'd have to resign from the fire department and tell my family goodbye. I'd have to leave behind the only place I've ever lived.

I would have to leave behind the only girl I've ever loved. And still love, desperately.

But this chance also gives me a new life. One without so much hurt or history. I could start a new chapter in St. Louis. Getting back into baseball might be the best thing for me.

When we'd ended the call, I'd told Daniel I needed a couple of weeks to think about it, consider the logistics of moving. Really, I just needed to sort my damn head out.

"Bowen, my boy!"

A familiar face walks through the door of my barbershop, and I at least have the politeness to fake a smile for him.

"Coach Hankins, good to see you." We shake hands, and he takes a seat in my chair.

"I look forward to coming in here every four weeks. Not only for my haircut but because I get to talk to you."

My old high school baseball coach is as good of a person as there comes. He's a stickler for discipline on the field, but he's fair. Coach Hankins has won the most baseball championships in Pennsylvania history in his twenty-two years running the program. And the reason he's so successful is that he coaches out of respect for his players, rather than leading with fear or intimidation.

"I will say I don't mind you as much as some other customers," I joke.

"But you'd rather talk to no one. I know you more than you remember, Bow." The old man flashes me a grin as I set a cape over his shoulders.

He doesn't have to tell me what we're doing, I've been straight buzzing Coach's head since I took over the business.

"How's the team looking for next season?" I ask, genuinely curious.

From time to time, my brothers and I will catch a game in town. We all played for Hankins, and I still do fundraisers with the team, as does Keaton.

"Eh, they're just okay, to be honest. Lots of heart, but no real superstars. My seniors who graduated last year were the big swingers, and the team will be hurting without them. But it's okay, heart is better than talent."

I nod. "Yes, it is."

The razor drowns out conversation for a little, and I focus all of my attention on shaping Coach's cut. My work might not be rocket science, but I'm good at it and it takes my mind away from my shitty reality at the moment.

Reaching for my comb to see if everything is even, Coach catches my eyes in the mirror.

"You know, Bowen, I'm an old man, now."

My grin is sly. "Are you trying to tell me something I don't know?"

"Shut it, boy." His voice is gruff but his eyes sparkle with laughter. "What I'm saying is, soon, it will be time for me to retire."

"I didn't realize you were thinking about it. Honestly, I thought you'd die in that dugout."

Coach Hankins chuckles. "Many people do, too. But nah. Marjorie is bugging me, says we need to spend some of our retirement together. And my bones are old, my heart is tired. I love coaching, but I just don't have the energy anymore. I have to find someone to fill my shoes."

I dust his neck off, unsuspecting when he hits me with his next choice of words.

"And looking in this mirror right now, I think you might be the best man for the job."

I nearly drop the razor I'm about to trim the last uneven bit of his hairline with. "Wh ... what?"

Coach laughs, a booming, jubilant sound coming from deep in his throat. "Don't swallow your tongue now, boy. And don't act so surprised. I'm in here a week early ... I think you're losing track of time."

Now that he says it ... I realize he's right. "You came in here to ask me to ... what exactly?"

"To become the coach of the Fawn Hill High School varsity baseball team." He smirks.

The idea gets my heart thumping, and my mouth going dry.

Coach removes his own cape, standing from the chair to check his new do out in the mirror.

"Great job, kid." He fishes in his wallet, gives me the usual fifteen dollars for the cut, and the fifteen-dollar tip.

I've told him a hundred times to stop tipping the same amount that I charge for the cut, that no one tips a hundred percent. He just smiles and whistles as he walks out, usually.

But this time, he turns to me. "I'll let you think about it. But I'd like to hang up my cleats sooner rather than later. Let me know, Bowen."

And then he leaves.

Jesus. That big decision just turned into a fucking *enormous* decision.

35

LILY

It takes me an entire day to pull myself out of bed.

That may not seem like much, but for me, it's monumental. Never in my life have I missed a day of work due to personal issues. I don't call out. I don't shuck responsibilities, or leave my friends hanging, or silence calls from my mother.

But ever since Bowen revealed the secret that made my world implode, all the pieces of my life have fallen by the wayside. When I left his house, I came straight home, crawled into bed, and haven't been out of it since.

I never understood how depression or bone-deep sadness can affect a person so brutally. You hear those stories or watch the recounting of someone who went through it and think: There is no way I'd ever be so sad that my body would simply shut down.

But it happens. It's like the body and mind's own way of doing damage control. Simply shutting off, not rebooting, not allowing you to explore a conscious state because if you do ... the pain you'll experience is too great to handle.

I thought sleep would evade me that I'd be crying into my pillow for hours on end. But the minute I pulled the comforter over me, the world went dark. Sleep consumed me, I'd wake for a hazy second and then be pulled back under.

When I finally surface long enough to check my cell on my nightstand, I realize I've been out for almost twenty-four hours. It's five p.m. the next day, and I have approximately seventy missed calls from Bowen, more texts, and thirty unread emails from work. Thank God I'd had the forethought to email my part-time employee to cover me before I went into my sleep coma.

That word choice is ironic, considering I'd been unconscious at the time Bowen was threatened to leave me ... and actually listened.

I couldn't believe it. Even as the truth rattles around in my brain now, the one thing I'd desperately wanted to know in the last ten years, I still don't believe it.

Our fathers. The actual men who had helped to create us ... wanted to keep us apart.

My father, the one who'd told me he loved me and wanted to see me succeed since the day I'd been born, had threatened and taken away the love of my life. He'd promised to expose the dirtiest, most vulgar part of our accident ... the reason why I wasn't wearing a seatbelt. A father, not to mention a stranger, should *never* hold that kind of information over their child's head. But mine did. Without me even knowing it.

I'm reeling and dizzy when I try to stand to head to the bathroom to empty my bulging bladder.

My eyes hurt as I turn on the lights in my house, the glow stinging my eyes. Every cell throbs with pain and exhaustion; I feel like I've simultaneously pulled an all-nighter and am coming off the worst hangover of my life.

There are so many things I want to do. My hands clench into fists as anger I've never experienced washes over my muscles. I want to break something, to hear the crunch of my knuckles against a hard surface.

I want to scream until my lungs are hoarse. I want to shed every tear behind my eyes. I want to demand answers from Bowen, ask why he followed their stupid rules, ask him why I wasn't enough to risk it all for.

But the thing I want to do most? I want to confront my goddamn father.

All I can manage to pull on are the closest sweatpants and shirt, my hair hanging limply around my face. I'm half-mad with delirium as I drive over to my parents, the route completely memorized as if it's on the back of my hand.

Most likely, I look like a disheveled vagabond when I stumble into their kitchen. It's dinnertime, and they're seated at the table, my father at the head and my mother sitting dutifully at his side.

"Why did you do it?" My finger points wildly in my father's direction, my voice unhinged.

If I was in the right frame of mind, I might have thought I needed to stew on this. To wait to confront him until I was presentable, until he couldn't refute me with his sly, underhanded tactics.

But I was raw, an open, beating vein that was gushing blood without any sign of stopping.

"Lily?" Mom rises from her chair, so much confusion in her eyes.

"You threatened him! Bowen. You told him to stay away from me." I can feel my eyes bulging out of their sockets.

My father, very calmly, wipes his mouth with his napkin. "Why, Lily, what a pleasant surprise."

There is nothing left of the father I knew. This man is evil ... power, greed, and control have gone to his brain and corrupted it.

"Don't do this. Don't lie. Give me the truth!" I scream, my brain unraveling. "You watched me fall apart for *months*. You've looked on as I've gone loveless and childless for *years*. Because Bowen is the only man I'll ever love, and yet you kept us separated for what? Because your ego couldn't handle a man who wasn't just like you being with your daughter? Because you deemed him too unworthy of me? Because he didn't fit into your perfect political family picture?"

This is it. I've finally snapped. Broken out of the chains my parents have placed on me from a young age. I'm no longer obedient, or speak only when spoken to, or put their needs and that of my father's career above my own. This betrayal, this absolute abuse of love and dedication ... it has destroyed us. Even further than my relationship with Bowen.

"Lily, what in the world?" My mom looks bewildered, shifting her eyes back and forth from my father and me.

"I have no idea what you're talking about." He has the audacity to sit there and deny this.

I feel like ripping my hair out, strand by strand. "You are my *father*. How could you do something like this?"

"If you've had some sort of fight with your ... *friend*, I don't see what that has to do with me. Other than I told you it would end badly."

My God, I might punch him. I've never felt this kind of anger toward a human.

"My *friend*? Bowen is the love of my life and a hell of a lot more of a man than you'll ever be. He was truly trying to protect me, from both your threats and from seeing what a horrible monster you are!"

I turn to my mother. "Bowen told me the reason he left. Why he's stayed away for ten years. It's because our fathers made a pact to keep us apart, and if either of us tried to get back together with the other, they'd expose secrets about us or try to tear us down. What would your husband have done to destroy me? His own daughter? He was going to let slip to everyone in town that the reason I was ejected from the car and ended up in a coma was because I was giving my boyfriend a hand job. There you go, the ugly truth. He is a monster, Mom, and I think you've seen it, too."

My mother's mouth falls open, the room going dead silent for a minute. The ticking hands on the clock over the kitchen sink are the only sounds for a full sixty seconds, and I know she's gone into shock.

I haven't though. For the first time in years, I have precise clarity.

"I am *done. Done.* I am no longer under your thumb, nor will I listen to your instructions or demands. Your life having a dutiful daughter, it is *over.*"

Pride, relief, sorrow, and anger mix like a lethal cocktail in my veins as I march for the front door. There is no more left to say, no more left to listen to. My father is not going to own up to this, nor will my mother give him the earful he deserves tonight.

The only thing left to do is go home and lick my wounds. Pick up the pieces of my life, throw the rotting ones away, and start anew with what little I have leftover.

36

BOWEN

I have never gone to my mother for advice or emotional support.

When I say never, I mean never.

First off, I'm a male. And I know that might be sexist, but unless we're really hard up about something, we most likely are not going to blab to our mama's about which girl broke our heart or what asshole friend stole our position on a sports team.

Now take that theory, multiply it by a hundred, and you get me.

Someone like Fletcher, he always indulged our mother in her need to gossip. She had no girls, and so someone had to fill it, and the most vulnerable of all of us was happy to do it. Keaton as well, as the oldest, went to her for a lot. Forrest, he was as lone wolf as they came, even in a family of five.

But me? I bottled everything up. I didn't rely on her for parental direction, and I think it had always caused a rift between us.

Except now I had a major dilemma weighing on me. More than one if I'm being honest. My head is so fucked up, I can barely see straight. And I need help.

I'm surprised when I end up on Mom's doorstep, but when she opens the door and greets me with a hug and a smile, I know instinctively that she'll make everything all right.

"Bowen!" she says as we end our quick hug. "What're you doing here? Who is at the shop?"

Mom might be more surprised than I am.

"I closed early for the day. Because ... because I need to talk." Those words sound strange coming out of my mouth.

And I've officially stunned my mother. "Oh ... okay. Of course, of course, uh, come in, dear."

She's flustered but excited, I think. It's taken almost thirty years for her middle son to come to her like this, so she's probably just as nervous as I am.

I tell her as much as we sit down in her living room. "I don't really know how to do this, truthfully."

Mom smiles, and I'm instantly calmed. "Well, start from the beginning, and I'll listen without interrupting."

That sounded fair enough. I lean down, my elbows on my knees, deciding where to start.

"I've been interviewing for positions in the baseball industry. Well, not interviewing for positions ... it's just one position. As a hitting coach for a minor league team in St. Louis. It would mean leaving Fawn Hill. Which is both terrifying, and something that could give me a fresh start. And then, just now, Coach Hankins walked into the barbershop and offered me the head coaching job at the high school, as he wants to retire. I don't even know if I'd be a good coach, and he's offering me the top spot. My own team, young minds I'd shape all on my own."

I stop for a second, gauging Mom's expression. She's listening intently, and when I don't continue, she motions for me to keep talking.

Her wrist rolls as her hand waves. "But? These are all good

things, Bowen. Tell me the big thing that determines it all. The one thing that makes your choice for you."

And now I hang my head. "Lily."

"Ah, I knew that was in there," Mom says quietly. "You love her."

I nod. "Always have. But ... we're through now."

"You're what?" Now my mother's voice gets a little screechy. "Why?"

This is the part I've been dreading, the part I never wanted to get to. I knew the minute I spilled my darkest secret to Lily that I'd also have to take it to my mother. Because I know, beyond a shadow of a doubt, that she never had any idea about the pact Dad made with Senator Grantham. When I tell her this, it will forever change the way she sees my father, and he's not here to explain or defend himself. Speaking ill of the dead is usually not a wise thing, but my mother needs to know the whole truth.

"Because I kept the ultimate secret from her. The one that has separated us since the accident." I take a deep breath, my stomach dropping as if I'm going over a cliff. "Dad made a promise with Senator Grantham, after our car crash. To keep us apart. To make sure that Lily and I, if we ever got back together ... that we'd both be destroyed. They made a pact of mutually assured destruction, to expose our deepest secrets and ruin both of our futures."

My mother's eyes glaze over with tears, and she redirects her gaze out the big bay window in her living room. Her reaction is immediate, and my mother would never dare question me on this. She knows how little I've come to her, which is basically never. If I'm admitting something this detrimental to her, it's not something I misheard or misunderstood because I was a teenager. My mother knows I'm telling the truth.

I hear her sniffle and see her shoulders shake. A lump of emotion forms in my throat, and I try to swallow it down. I've always been the one who needs her the least ... and to come to her with this? It's so unlike the relationship we have.

Growing up, I was always the independent one. Yes, most people would say that's Forrest now, but I don't mean the loner. I mean independent. Forrest and Fletcher were the babies, and twins at that, they needed her full attention for most of my childhood. Keaton was the oldest, and therefore her golden boy. He was the first, the one who made her a mom.

Don't feel sorry for me, I don't care about being the middle child. My mother and I just have a different relationship than my brothers do with her. But I still love her and keeping this secret for this long was not fair to her.

Mom shakes her head, turning back to look into my eyes. "Your father was a wonderful man. And at the same time, he made some terrible decisions. If that man wasn't already in heaven ..."

I look away, both ashamed that I never told her, and ashamed that I'm telling her something damaging after he's gone. My conflicting emotions about my dad, ever since the day he told me about the pact he'd made with Lily's father, have haunted me immensely after his death.

On one hand, he loved his family and would do anything to protect us. On the other, he took away the only thing I had left to live for after the accident. He altered the trajectory of my life forever.

Her small, warm hands grab my large ones, and the difference is stark. "Bowen, look at me."

I do, because I'd never disobey her. This woman is the strongest person I've ever known.

"Your father was wrong. And God rest his soul ... but he was wrong to do that to you. To make decisions like that, to give in to that horrible man's threats. His protective instinct was misguided, and he wronged you. He took away the one person you loved most, even more than your brothers or me. I watched as you sat next to her bed day in and day out. Even while your world was imploding, you always stood by her side. You're an amazing man, you were then and you are now. Do not let the mistakes of your father ruin the future you still have left."

And now I break down. Because finally, one of my parents sees my pain. My mother is acknowledging me, just as I am, and she's given me the outlet to lose it. Tears stream from my eyes, all the unspeakable words trapped inside my chest and my head flow out as silent sobs wrack my shoulders.

Mom huddles close, holding me to her, as she rubs my back and whispers that it's all going to be okay.

After what feels like an eternity, I straighten, collecting myself. "Tell me what to do."

Her smile is knowing, and small. "I can't tell you what to do. But I can tell you what *I* think. What to do, that's all up to you. I think that you've loved Lily for your whole life. And you made a tough decision after a very influential person in your life made a *wrong* decision. But you're still a young man. You have so many years ahead. Don't waste them by not going after her. Now that there are no secrets between you, put it all out on the line."

"But the senator ... he still could—"

"He could still what, sweetheart? It's been ten years, you're a grown man, Lily is her own woman ... no matter how much he tries to control her. I think you've both paid a high enough price. There is nothing he can do to bring you down anymore. And if he tries, he'll have to go through me. Your father may have let you down, but I'll jump in front of a bullet for any of my boys. The big bad senator doesn't scare me."

I have to snort out a laugh at her. "What about the position in St. Louis?"

Mom's face grows somber. "All I can say about that is ... if that's what your heart is telling you to do, I won't hold you back.

But I'll throw my weight around here because I want all of my boys close to me. Fawn Hill is your home. And you have a perfectly good opportunity to keep your shop, be involved in baseball, and still work with the fire department. Right here, you have *all* of that. If you want to spread your wings, I won't stop you. I've only ever wanted what's best for you. Especially you, Bowen. I think you forget sometimes that Lily wasn't the only one gravely injured in that accident."

It's going to take some time for me to digest everything that has happened here today.

So for now, I take her hands in mine and squeeze. "Thank you for listening."

"Thank you for coming to me. I'll admit, I've been waiting for a day like this. I'm not happy about the news you brought, but I'm happy it brought you, at least, to open up."

37

LILY

A week goes by, October ends, and the uncertainty that has settled over my life has me waking in the middle of the night, *every* night.

By the eighth night, as I stare at the clock on my bedside table, which reads 1:06 a.m., I'm so over this shattering heartbreak that I roll my eyes.

When will it pass?

I used to ask myself this a lot after I came out of the coma. When will the pain pass? When will I get better? When will I stop loving him?

That last question ... I never answered it. Because I still haven't stopped, not even now when he brought my whole world crashing down over my head.

In my mind, I know that Bowen was just as trapped in the decisions of our fathers as I was. He was a pawn in their game, too, and was only trying to protect me. I believe him when he says that. But it still cuts deep, knowing that he knew about it and I was left in the dark. If he'd only told me, if we'd only been able to discuss it and come up with a plan ...

We wouldn't have wasted so much time.

My heart squeezes, an ache I can't rub out of my chest that twinges every time I think about all the wasted years. It's just a damn shame.

Rubbing my eyes, I get out of bed, slip into clothes, and go downstairs to pull my long, black goose down coat over it all. With my feet in boots, I lock my front door and begin to walk.

Most sane people wouldn't dare venture out into the thirty-degree night at one a.m., and they'd be completely right not to. But this was Fawn Hill. Crime here was nonexistent, and I'd been surviving the cold of rural Pennsylvania for as long as I could remember.

I needed a sign, some kind of answer. And so I was going back to the spot where I might find one.

Bloomsbury Park comes into view quicker than I anticipated, or maybe I'm just walking fast because I'm freezing my buns off. It's so quiet and almost smells of snow, and my heart skips a beat thinking about the holidays. This time is my favorite, how Thanksgiving blends right into Christmas and then it's a new year.

And then I realize ... I won't have anyone to spend them with. My family ... well, my parents, they're not really my family anymore. I won't be acting out our traditions anymore.

So what will I do?

I'm thinking about it as I come upon the gazebo. *Our* gazebo. Thoughts of how I'll spend the holidays alone like that song by The Waitresses distract me as I walk up the steps.

It's not until I'm standing fully under the vaulted ceiling that I realize ...

Bowen is right in front of me.

"*Lily* ..." he breathes, his voice awestruck.

"What are you ...?" The words come before I can stop them.

And then I realize, I came here for a sign. Well, universe, if this isn't the most obvious sign *ever*.

His baby blues are trained on me. "I've been coming here every night since you left. Hoping against hope that you'd show up. And if you didn't, hoping that being here would bring me the strength to fight for us. To get you back even if you came at me swinging."

"I would never swing at you," I say quietly.

He shrugs, a small smile turning up those stubble-covered cheeks. "I wouldn't blame you if you did."

Neither of us speaks, and I wrap my puffy-coated arms around myself.

"Lily, I am so sorry. I hate those words because they don't mean enough. I wish I could ... I don't know, rip out my heart or something to show you just how sorry I am. To show you that my intentions were good, but my actions were terrible. I know that you might not want to hear this, but I love you so much and—"

I hold up a hand for him to stop. "I'm hurt. I'm angry. You kept me out of the decision-making process on the only decision that mattered. *Us*. You decided for me how we would end, and I wasn't even privy to why. You wasted so much time, Bowen ... *years* that we can't get back."

And now the tears come. Silent at first, but then ugly, ricocheting through my chest as I try to speak. He's right there, so close to me, in *our* place. How I got out of bed, walked here, and found him ... it can only be blamed on something bigger than both of us. And when he steps into the light, I see the tears in *his* eyes.

My breath whistles through my teeth as I suck it in sharply. I've never seen Bowen cry in my entire life. I don't know if he ever has in his entire life. But here he is, this rugged, aggressive man, standing in front of me with tears about to fall.

That's when I crack.

"I know you were trying to protect me ... I do know that. But we were partners, Bowen. I wasn't just in love with you like some lustful high school girl. You were my *best friend*. We'd talked about making life decisions together. You were *my person*. And in an instant, you doubted that and let other people influence what happened to us. And still, I love you more than any of those other emotions. I love you even when I hate you. I love you even when you betray me so fatally it feels like you've opened a vein and drained it."

He touches me. Bowen pulls me in so close that I think he feels if he doesn't grasp me the hardest he can, I'll slip through his fingers.

It makes me weak, but it also makes me infinitely stronger. In his arms, with him in my life and giving me just as much love as I can give him ... it's how we can move past this. It's how I'll rise again, how I can live.

Over the past week, I've thought a lot about what a person who loves you looks like. How you can spot the real, genuine kind, and how you know they'll go to the ends of the earth for you because of that love. Bowen is that kind of person. He sacrificed himself for me. His life, his dreams, his shot at our life together.

"I chose wrong once. I will never do that again. Because this time, I choose you. Above all else, above family, and jobs, and especially fear ... I choose you, Lily. I love you. I'll love you forever. Please, tell me you want the same."

My eyes shift quickly, back and forth, as I try to take in all of his face with my gaze. I want to remember this moment. The one that ends our long tale of turmoil and heartbreak.

"Of course, that's what I want. I would choose a lifetime with you over and over again, no matter the consequences."

There, in the middle of our spot, Bowen kisses me.

It's *the* kiss, the one that seals us from now until the end of our days. The one that says more than any syllable could.

The one that puts every bad decision and source of heartbreak behind us.

From this moment on, we are together.

38

BOWEN

"Did you do it in the gazebo again?"

Fletcher smirks at me from across the barbershop as he flips through a magazine from the waiting area table.

"Dude, it was like negative twenty degrees. Without a doubt, they didn't fuck in the park. Bowen's dick would have frozen off," Forrest answers for me, rolling his eyes.

"Keep your head straight." I push his neck down. "I should give you an uneven cut for how fucking annoying you've been during this."

"Then you wouldn't earn your tip," he singsongs.

"As if you pay me anyway, freeloader." I do the last few touchups on his hair and then smack him before I take the cape off. "Who told you two about the gazebo anyway?"

"About you losing your virginity? We read it in your diary." Fletcher snickers.

"What the hell! I was talking about how Lily and I made up the other night in the gazebo. Who told you about losing our virginity?" Now I'm pissed because someone has been blabbing.

"Keaton. Never tell him anything. He tried to use it with us as a safe sex speech when we turned sixteen." Forrest snorts.

"Like that worked." Fletcher fist bumps his twin as they meet up by the cash out counter.

I have to breathe through my nose to keep calm around these two. "I swear, you two are the ones making me go gray."

"Always worried about your precious hair." Fletcher laughs.

The bell over my shop door tinkles, and in walks the most gorgeous surprise I've ever seen.

"Oh ... hey, everyone. Didn't realize you two would be here as well." Lily smiles at my brothers, and they both walk over to kiss her on the cheek.

She's dressed in work attire; tight polka-dotted black pants and a bright red V-neck sweater. It's innocent, subtly sexy, and she's making my mouth water.

And because I've already wasted enough time, I march my ass right on across my barbershop and scoop her up in my arms as I crush my mouth to hers.

Lily lets out a yelp of excitement and surprise that I promptly swallow. I feel it when she melts into the kiss, involuntarily giving over control as I pry at the seam of her mouth with my tongue.

"Um, should we just go?" Forrest's rude voice interrupts us.

My girl jumps in my arms, and I know that I made her forget we were in other people's company. I beam with pride.

"Oh, I'm sorry ..." She giggles, covering her bruised lips. "I just came by to bring Bowen lunch, but I have to get back to the library in like ... well, actually now."

"A girl who brings you lunch? I have to get me one of those." Fletcher pouts.

I point my finger at him. "You have to get you no such thing. A year of sobriety, that means girls, too."

We didn't need him backsliding because an emotion as fickle as love got involved.

He produces something from his pocket. "I guess my ban is up, then. Got my one year chip the other day."

"Fletcher! That is amazing." Lily walks away from me to go envelop him in a hug.

"Wow, I ... didn't realize. I'm proud of you." I nod at him.

"All right, I really do have to go, though. Just wanted to come see your face for a minute. I'll see you tonight, yeah?" Lily crosses the room back toward me.

"I wouldn't want to be anywhere else." I pull her in once more, breathing a full lungful of her in. I have to have a hit to get me through the rest of my day.

I watch her all the way down the block, like a lovesick puppy standing at my shop windows waiting for her to return.

"You've got it bad." Forrest pats my shoulder as he passes and walks out.

Fletcher salutes and follows his brother, and I'm alone.

They're right ... I do have it bad. Always have, always will, and I'm no longer afraid to admit that. In fact, I'm downright proud of it.

It's as if everything that existed before, the hurt, secrets, heartbreak, loss ... it all got erased that night in the gazebo. There was an unspoken agreement between Lily and me that from here on out, we were moving forward. The storm clouds that had occupied the space above our heads, and in our hearts, were finally gone.

And I might be riding the high of our makeup sex, which had been going strong for the last week, but this was the happiest I'd been in my entire life. Even more than our glory days when I still had a chance at going to the majors. This was better than that because this was real. Back then, we thought we were wild and free, but we didn't know anything.

We were grown-ups now, and Lily and I could do whatever we wanted. Have sleepovers every night. Move in together. Get married. Have babies.

Of course, I hadn't proposed all of those ideas yet, but I had a feeling she wouldn't want to wait. Just as much as I didn't want to wait.

We'd lost enough time. We had a lot of catching up to do.

39

LILY

The weeks leading up to Thanksgiving are chock full of quality time with Bowen.

Friday nights at the Fawn Hill movie theater, nighttime walks to our gazebo, Saturday mornings spent in bed and him driving me to work more than once or twice a week. We spend every night and day at each other's houses, and by the Tuesday before the holiday, Bowen is trying to convince me to move in with him.

"But ... I like my townhouse better. Look how cute it is. How about you just move in here?"

"Well, for starters, I have my punching bag set up in my basement. And I need that. Plus, I have more room." He adjusts on the couch, pulling me farther into him.

Even though we are basically already laying on top of each other.

"I'm not crazy about your setup ... and those floors, yuck." I place a chaste kiss on his cheek.

Bowen shrugs. "So gut the place. Room by room. Do whatever you want. Just move in with me."

I'm a little shocked as I turn to him. "You'd really let me do that?"

"Yes. All I care is that I go to sleep next to you every night and wake up to you every morning. I don't care what the walls and carpets surrounding us look like. But if you do, then change them. I want you to be happy, that's all I want."

And because I'm saying yes to everything these days, especially when it comes to Bowen, I agree. "Okay. When can I move in?"

He jumps up. "Right now. Let's go out and get some boxes."

That makes me giggle. "Hold your horses, speed demon. I have to sell this place."

"And you can move in with me while we list it. It'll make it a hundred times easier to show if no one is living here. Come on!"

A sound from the front hallway has my words freezing in my throat. Because I can swear that sounds like a key.

Bowen's eyes take in my body language, he hears the noise, and I watch him go into full protection mode. If I wasn't so freaked out myself, I'd be in awe of this pure show of masculinity.

"Lily."

I suck a breath in because the voice coming from the entryway of my townhouse is one I know.

Even if it's one I never wanted to hear again.

"What are you doing here?" My tone is ice as I stand, and my father enters the living room.

He holds up one hand, a smug, almost condescending look on his face. "I just came to talk."

"He still has a key?" Bowen growls, his eyes never leaving mine.

"I forgot." Which only makes me feel unsafe.

Imagine that? Feeling unsafe when it comes to your parent, your blood relative.

"Get out," Bowen tells him now, moving in front of me.

Protecting me, as he has always tried to do.

"You get away from my daughter!" Dad sneers, rounding my coffee table and storming toward Bowen.

My father is not a man who likes to be told what to do, and from the moment he waltzed in here, uninvited, you could feel the shift in the air. He was looking for a fight.

"Dad! What are you doing?" I shout, trying to throw myself in front of the man I love.

"We had a deal, your father and I, and that doesn't change because he dropped dead." My father points his finger past my ear, straight into Bowen's face.

Behind me, I hear Bowen snarl, and I can feel the fury rolling off him in scorching waves.

Finally, my father is admitting it. He wouldn't do it in front of Mom when I went postal on them in their kitchen. No, he waited until he could sneak in and spook me. It spoke volumes about his character.

"That is horrible, how could you talk like that! After everything you've put us through." I choke on the last few words.

"You should have just left us be. We're happy ... we love each other. Why has that always been so hard for you to accept?" Bowen's hand laces through mine, and I instantly feel stronger.

"Keep your hands off her. The last time you couldn't manage to, she almost died." There is murder in my father's eyes.

"Stop it! The deal is broken, it's over. Do your worst, but don't lie to him or me. We both know the truth. We've worked past the hurt, something you clearly can't do and don't want to. That accident was just that ... an accident. Everything that happened after—my pain, heartbreak, years of unrequited love and so much damage done—that was on you. If anything died here, it was our relationship. Yours and mine."

I'm shaking so hard that Bowen has to physically hold me to him to keep me from collapsing to the floor.

"You took your seatbelt off to ... like some kind of harlot. You almost got yourself killed trying to hook up with your cocky, idiotic athlete boyfriend. How would that have looked to the press? The constituents. That the daughter of a senator couldn't keep it in her pants long enough to not be ejected from the passenger seat."

The devil stands before me, red-faced and spiraling, spewing out hate and venom.

"Get out of my house." My voice is deadly calm, and I stand hand in hand with Bowen.

My protector doesn't curl his body around me though, no ... he lets me stand strong and independent.

"Lily, he's trash. A barber, nowhere near what you deserve or the kind of man—"

"You have no idea what kind of man he is. And I don't need to prove to you how worthy he is of me. If anything, I'm not worthy of him. He has spent years ripping out his own heart over and over and over again because of something *you* did. Because he wanted the best for me even if that meant it couldn't be him. I said get out of my house. So go. *Now*."

My father backs away slowly, his eyes boring holes into the both of us.

"Wait," Bowen demands. "Leave her key."

He throws it, basically spits it back at us. "Keep it. I don't need to associate with trash. Even if she is my own daughter."

That was meant as an insult, but surprisingly, I feel nothing. His words hold no weight anymore, and thus, they can't hurt me.

As soon as we hear the front door click closed, Bowen moves swiftly to lock it.

And then he's right back at my side, wrapping me in his arms. "Are you okay?"

My eyes look up into his. "Yes ... yes, I think I am. A little shaken, but ... he admitted to it. That's what I wanted. Now we can ... we can move on from this."

"Let's go back to my place. Our place. Move in with me, *tonight*."

He doesn't have to ask me twice. "How fast can we pack?"

40
LILY

I wake to Bowen's hands trailing down my body.

"What're you doing?" I yawn on the tail end of a smile.

"It's Thanksgiving. I'm trying to show you what I'm *most* thankful for," he says as his fingers push past the elastic band of my underwear.

"Mmm." I get temporarily distracted as they brush the bundle of nerves above my opening. "We have to get up. I promised your Mom I would help her get the turkey in."

Bowen nibbles my earlobe between his teeth. "Sh, I'm working here."

He presses the blunt tip of his finger into my core, circling in a delicious motion that has me squirming. A moan escapes my lips, and I reach behind me, my hands caressing his muscled thighs. They drag up to his waist and contort to reach inside his boxers, where I find him hard and leaking for me.

I never can resist him.

"Hmm, yeah, babe." He gasps into my hair as I circle around him, squeezing tighter as I pull toward his head.

In just a couple of seconds, we go from lazily teasing to panting, and Bowen flips me over shortly after.

"I love you." He grunts as he pushes into me, our naked flesh tangling.

"I love you," I answer, reaching up to thread my arms around his neck.

He makes slow, seductive love to me, quietly in the sanctuary of our shared bedroom. The build-up is agonizing, with each stroke, each gasp, each tense pulse of our bodies. When my orgasm finally washes over me, my mind is numb and my limbs quake with the blissful electricity buzzing through them.

Bowen covers my lips with his, groaning into my throat as his climax leaves him breathless.

We lay entwined, silent but for the labored breaths of our post-coital glow, for what feels like an hour.

"That was the perfect start to Thanksgiving morning. I think we just made a new tradition." Bowen smiles into my neck, breaking the quiet.

I plant a kiss on his cheek and push on his chest for him to let me up. "I agree. But right now, we have to get ready."

"A drill sergeant, you are. I think we need to talk about how bossy you are."

"You like it." I grin as I walk to the bathroom.

I hear him shuffling around in the bedroom while I pee, brush my hair, rinse with mouthwash and begin to apply the light amount of makeup I wear each day. He comes in looking like some fall catalog model out of a J. Crew ad. Olive green chunky knit sweater, dark blue jeans, cognac-colored boots, and his hair perfectly, sexily mussed from sex.

I'd say it isn't fair to be that good looking, but I get to reap the rewards from it so I'm not complaining.

"Hi, gorgeous." I raise a brow.

Bowen blushes, which is so rare, but I love making him do it. "So you're going over to help Mom with the turkey while Keaton and I grab the pies from the bakery?"

I glance down at my hands. "Um, yeah, that was the plan. But I'm wondering if you could drop me somewhere else first."

"Sure, where?" His voice is unsuspecting.

"I wanted to go see my mom." I look up guiltily.

When he doesn't answer, his expression unreadable, I continue. "It's just ... it's Thanksgiving. I haven't spoken to her since the truth about what my father did came out. I know it's probably weak to want to see her, but I spent twenty-seven years with her on this day. I just kind of want to go see her."

Bowen crouches down in front of me where I sit at the makeshift vanity I set up. "Lily, that's not weak. It's called love, and I think it's admirable. Of course, I'll drop you off to see your mom."

My boots crunch on the leaves littering the sidewalk as I near the street where Eliza bought her townhouse.

I decided to walk from my parent's house to Bowen's mother's place, to clear my head. And because I didn't want to sit in a car and dissect the conversation with him just yet.

It had been strange being back in my mother's house after the blow that happened there. It was almost a month ago, but it felt like yesterday. Thank God my father hadn't been there today, something I'd been counting on as I'd checked his schedule and he was out of town. That's right, out of town on the first Thanksgiving my mother wasn't going to be spending the holiday with me. The man had no heart.

Our conversation had been odd and stiff, there was too much hurt between us now. In the past, I'd unconsciously forgiven my mother for turning the other cheek when my father did questionable things, but now it almost added to how badly he'd betrayed me. She claims she knew nothing about what he did after the accident, but I'm not sure I can believe that.

The mother I knew, the one who supported me and loved me with such an open and big heart ... I wasn't sure she could be trusted anymore.

And that was a shame. Decades of a relationship built, shattered because of one monumental lie.

As I push through the screen door, my mind is temporarily distracted from the sadness of my own family. The Nash's buzz about the first floor, cooking, singing, setting the table, and especially drinking.

Forrest is passing out beers while Presley pours a red, steaming liquid into a bowl.

"It's mulled wine!" she says excitedly to Hattie, her grandmother, and then looks up to see me standing in the room. "Lily! Bowen, Lily is here!"

My man rounds the corner and smiles a mega-watt smile. "Welcome to chaos!"

He's so jubilant, it's contagious. We meet in the middle of the room, our kiss sweet and happy. Then Bowen takes me by the hand, pulling me into a quieter side hallway.

"How was your mother?" His tone holds something back, and I know he's trying to allow me to talk without prying too much.

I wrap my arms around his waist and bury my head in his T-shirt. Because I can do that now, touch him whenever I want with no reason or backlash at all.

"She was okay. It was ... not an easy talk, to say the least. I'm still not convinced she didn't know, although she swears it. Says she hasn't even spoken to Dad in two weeks, although they're staying together. That much is clear. She'll always be the good wife; they've been through too much now. To me, this is the worst betrayal, but I ... I think she knows where the bodies are buried. They're a team, which I guess is admirable. It's just ... it's all so messed up, Bow."

He pulls me in tighter, raining kisses down on my cheeks. "I know it is. I feel the same way. My father isn't here to answer for his wrong-doings, and I know you don't even want to hear it from yours."

"It's like ... I'm furious at him for keeping us apart, for making me lose ten years that I could have had with you. But at the same time ... in an adult sense, I can see how our fathers wanted to protect us. It might have been a convoluted way of doing it, but ..."

I trail off and he tips my chin up with two fingers, those blue eyes searching mine. "What, baby?"

"My mom said something a while back. She said that even though they were our parents, they were still people. They had flaws, made mistakes. Maybe that's why I'm allowing forgiveness to sit side by side with my fury."

Bowen swipes his thumb across my cheek. "How do you always know what I'm thinking?"

"Because I'm in love with you."

He kisses me, and there has never been anything sweeter to taste. The freedom of doing this whenever I feel like it ... it's going to take some getting used to. In fact, I think I'll need to try it out over and over again.

"Do you think ... do you think you'll talk to your father?" Bowen pulls his mouth away from mine.

I sigh, exhausted from the whole thing. If I had a dollar for how many times I didn't want to think about any of it anymore.

"Right now, absolutely not. After the stunt he pulled at my townhouse ... I'm pretty sure our relationship is irreparable. It will only lead to more anger. My mother was trying to reason with me, to see his side of things, but this close, I can't rationalize anything he did. I need to make sense of my feelings in the situation, and eventually, maybe. But right now, it's a hard no."

Bowen's eyes narrow, but he still keeps me in his arms. "And I guess I'll have to respect that. How are you so much more mature than me?"

"I think it may have something to do with my anatomy." I wink.

"Mmm, you may be right. Care to test the theory … again?"

When Bowen bends down to kiss me, I dodge him. "I have a turkey to prepare."

As he chases me through the hall, into the kitchen where his family is busying themselves with food, I laugh.

Because I let him catch me. Because I've been chased into a place which is right where I want to be.

41

BOWEN

"Opening presents on Christmas Eve? We're going to have to talk about that."

I tickle Lily's side gently as she takes a seat on the rug next to me, with Presley on her other side.

"Well, it was only me, and in the morning we always went to church. I'm not saying I'm not willing to change traditions. Or create ones of our own."

"I like the sound of that." My hands bury in her hair as I kiss her.

"Hey, no funny business during the Christmas Eve movie!" Forrest scolds us.

Mom chuckles where she sits on the couch, next to Fletcher. The dog that Presley and Keaton recently adopted, a golden retriever with a soft spot for his grandma, lies between us. Forrest is in one of the armchairs, and Hattie in the other, with my girlfriend and I next to my brother and his wife on the floor.

We're all in matching Christmas pajamas, something that Lily and Presley forced us into. But, if you held my hand to a hot stovetop, I'd have to admit it's kind of fun.

"What are we watching tonight?" Lily asks.

"The same movie we always watch on Christmas Eve. But for you newbies, it's a surprise," Fletcher answers.

Mom gets up to do the honors of setting up the DVD, something she had to learn after Dad passed and she took the duty from him. I push that sadness out of my mind and stand up.

"Actually, I have one announcement before we start." I clear my throat, and my family looks at me expectantly. "I wanted to let you all know that, uh, Coach Hankins offered me the head coach position after he retires this June. And ... I decided to take it. So, I'm going to be the baseball coach at the high school."

Lily nods reassuringly, her beautiful smile beaming just for me.

We've talked about this at length over the last two months. After extending the deadline on the St. Louis job, which Daniel was very patient about, I wanted to include her in the decision-making process. After all, she was going to be the biggest part of my life. Lily insisted she didn't mind moving, that it might give us a new start. And we both really did consider what life might be like if we left Fawn Hill.

But in the end, both of us just couldn't do it. We agreed that this was our home, that our friends and family meant too much. And with an opportunity right in town to coach baseball, why would we even need to leave?

I'd told Coach Hankins last week I'd be honored to assume his duties as head coach, and he'd taken a bottle of whiskey out of his desk drawer and poured me a mug full to celebrate. It was still six months off, and a whole school year of sports seasons away, but I was damn excited.

"Oh, Bowen, I'm so happy that's what you decided." Mom comes at me with open arms, her small body wrapping me up in a tight bear hug.

Keaton uncurls from Presley and stands, offering me a clap on the back. "You'll make a great coach, brother."

"Imagine all the shithead teens you'll have to put up with. I know Coach Hankins almost ran me over with his truck he was so annoyed at me most times." Forrest cackles, but fist bumps me.

Fletcher comes over to make the hug Mom is giving me a group hug. "I'm proud of you, bro."

He's probably thinking about how much guidance Hankins gave him in the past. I only hope I can live up to our old coach's reputation.

"All right, all right, can we please start the movie?" Forrest whines.

We all grumble at him, but settle back into our spots, under blankets, cuddling our loved ones. It's the perfect representation of what I want for my life. What I want for our life, mine and Lily's. She doesn't know it yet, but one of those presents under our tree at home, the ones we'll open on Christmas *morning*, is a diamond ring.

I'm going to ask her to marry me tomorrow.

Mom pops the DVD in the player just under her TV, and the opening title for *It's a Wonderful Life* paints the screen.

And it is. Such a wonderful life.

EPILOGUE
LILY

Five Years Later

Sweet, cotton-candy sugared air wafts over the park, the summer wind carrying the scent of the carnival with it.

I sit on a blanket on the ground, my legs crossed at the ankles as I squint into the sun.

Our daughter runs to me, her little three-and-a-half-year-old legs chugging fast.

"Mommy! Aunt Penelope was kissing Uncle—"

"Hey, you know what I say about snitches!" Bowen interrupts her, scooping her up into an upside down hold.

She giggles loudly as he blows raspberries onto her belly, and I marvel at the similarities between them. Molly is every ounce of her father; dark hair, almost black, bright blue eyes, a stubborn personality and has absolutely no fear.

"They get stitches!" Molly tucks her hair behind her ears as he sets her back on her feet.

"That's right." Bowen fist bumps her, and I can't help but laugh at their ridiculousness.

"The things you teach this kid." I roll my eyes.

"Oh, you love it. And I'm going to teach all the same things to little man here." Bowen reaches down, rubbing my big baby belly.

His wedding ring glints as he smooths his hand over the place his son currently occupies, and I shift uncomfortably as said boy kicks at my internal organs.

"Any day now, I feel it." I huff out a breath.

If my husband had his way, we'd have six little ones toddling around by now. But I wanted to plan a real wedding after he proposed on Christmas, and it took us almost a year to save up. And once we'd had Molly, I wanted to enjoy motherhood and give her time to be the baby before we added another to the mix. Turns out, being a mom is even better than I thought it would be.

I've cut back at the library and only work part-time now. Eliza watches Molly the two days I'm at work, and we explore Fawn Hill on the other three days. We even do mommy and me yoga with Presley and her one-year-old son, Maxwell, on Thursdays.

Bowen is busier than ever at the shop, and in his fourth year as the head baseball coach at the high school. Between his customers and the pressure of adding to the two championships he won back-to-back in the last two seasons, he's a constant ball of energy. There is something I never thought I'd say about Bowen. But with his schedule, he was forced, and coerced by me, to give up firefighting. I couldn't stand it when he went out on the few calls he got after we were married. I had flashbacks of the night I fell asleep on his porch, and I don't think I could suffer through that kind of anxiety forever.

Watching him as a father ... it's been magical. Molly has him wrapped around her little finger, and when I walk in to her putting butterfly clips in his hair, I know it's real love. Bowen won't let anyone touch his hair ... except for our girl.

"The monster has come for you!" Fletcher runs at Molly, scooping her up biting her little legs as he spins her upside down.

She giggles wildly. "Monsta! Monsta!"

Bowen and I laugh because she also has her uncles wrapped around her finger. Fletcher and Forrest have really melted, becoming fun uncles who will let her ride them around like petting zoo animals. Forrest Nash, ladies and gentlemen, lets my daughter use him as a zoo animal. He's really changed since falling for the woman who tamed him.

"Did you see your mom is here? Working the rotary club tent?" Bowen leans in when Fletcher carts our girl off, probably taking her to get something that will spoil her dinner.

I nod, leaning into him as he begins to massage my shoulders. "We talked for a minute. She was happy to see Molly."

I'd love to say that my parents and I fixed our relationship, but truthfully, it's still just as awkward as it was five years ago. Bowen and I don't speak about my dad, or to him, and he has only met Molly once. From what I can gather, he spends most of his time in Washington, and his marriage to my mother is still there but severely broken.

The light in my mother's eyes is dimmer than it once was. I almost feel sorry for her, but then I remember how much she aided in my father's change. How she stood beside him as he morphed into an evil man. She could have left him, over the last five years, and I would have welcomed her with open arms. But she gave up her relationship with her child over her relationship with her husband and being a mother now, I couldn't imagine ever doing that.

I love Bowen with my whole heart, but Molly is my everything. She takes precedence over all.

"Well, at least she got to see her for a little." Bowen is trying to change the subject, and I'm appreciative of it. "So, what does my wife want to eat?"

"I'd love a whole plate of funnel cake, but I'm afraid it won't fit. I'm not even hungry anymore, which is sad. This kid is going to be a bowling ball by the time he comes out."

"I can't wait to see him. You think he'll be another me clone?" He smirks.

I roll my eyes. "Hopefully, my genes will stick on this one. But if he does look exactly like you, we're in trouble. He's going to break *all* the hearts."

"Nah, he'll fall in love with one magnificent girl and be hooked on her forever." Bowen nuzzles my cheek, his fingers working magic on the knots in my back.

"Mm, sounds familiar. Tell me more about this undying love," I joke as we watch Molly running back toward us.

She crashes into my lap with a thud, jostling her brother in my belly, and begins to climb me to get to her daddy. When she does, she kisses Bowen on the lips, and then plants one on me, too.

This is our family, the one we've created out of the ashes of our storied past. And it might have hurt, it might have been incredibly hard, but I'd walk through it all again to get to this place.

The one where we're in love, united, and raising our babies.

After all was forgiven, what's left is love. And love with Bowen is all I've ever wanted.

Looking for more Nash Brothers? Read Flutter to see the sparks between Forrest and Penelope!

Read the rest of the Nash Brothers series, available now!

Fleeting
Forgiven
Flutter
Falter

ALSO BY CARRIE AARONS

Do you want your **FREE** Carrie Aarons eBook?

All you have to do is sign up for my newsletter, and you'll immediately receive your free book!

Then, check out all of my books, available in Kindle Unlimited!

Standalones:

If Only in My Dreams

Foes & Cons

Love at First Fight

Nerdy Little Secret

That's the Way I Loved You

Fool Me Twice

Hometown Heartless

The Tenth Girl

You're the One I Don't Want

Privileged

Elite

Red Card

Down We'll Come, Baby

As Long As You Hate Me

On Thin Ice

All the Frogs in Manhattan

Save the Date

Melt

When Stars Burn Out

Ghost in His Eyes

Kissed by Reality

The Prospect Street Series:

Then You Saw Me

The Callahan Family Series:

Warning Track

Stealing Home

Check Swing

Control Artist

Tagging Up

The Rogue Academy Series:

The Second Coming

The Lion Heart

The Mighty Anchor

The Nash Brothers Series:

Fleeting

Forgiven

Flutter

Falter

The Flipped Series:

Blind Landing

Grasping Air

The Captive Heart Duet:

Lost

Found

The Over the Fence Series:

Pitching to Win

Hitting to Win

Catching to Win

Box Sets:

The Nash Brothers Box Set

The Complete Captive Heart Duet

The Over the Fence Box Set

ABOUT THE AUTHOR

Author of romance novels such as Fool Me Twice and Love at First Fight, Carrie Aarons writes books that are just as swoon-worthy as they are sarcastic. A former journalist, she prefers the love stories of her imagination, and the athleisure dress code, much better.

When she isn't writing, Carrie is busy binging reality TV, having a love/hate relationship with cardio, and trying not to burn dinner. She lives in the suburbs of New Jersey with her husband, two children and ninety-pound rescue pup.

Please join her readers group, Carrie's Charmers, to get the latest on new books, exclusive excerpts and fun giveaways.

You can also find Carrie at these places:
Website
Amazon
Facebook
Instagram
TikTok
Goodreads

Made in United States
North Haven, CT
24 August 2022